WILD ABOUT DENALI

A Sweet Romantic Comedy

SARA BLACKARD

Chapter One

-*DREW*-

My phone rings my mum's tone, and I'm hesitant to answer. Not because I don't love my mum. She's pretty amazing. I'm just not sure I'm up for her inquisition about my return to Oz. But it's my mum, so I gird my loins and what not, and answer.

"I found the perfect spot for your rescue, honey. It's practically in the middle of the outback. You'd be out woop woop, just like you like, and the buildings are in good shape." My relentless mum starts right off without even a g'day.

I'm glad she didn't video chat so I don't have to hide the roll of my eyes. I love her. She's the best. Raised me all on her lonesome once my deadbeat dad left us for another woman. Lately, though, every conversation circles back to this. Her latest property find as she scours Australia for a place for the animal rescue I want to open. Me, letting her down … again.

"No, Mum, I'm not coming back to Oz." I turn to the floor to ceiling windows that overlook Resurrection

Bay in Seward, Alaska. "In fact, I've found where I want to open up, even have an appointment with the realtor this arvo."

I glance at my watch. Good, it's only noon. The meeting's not until two followed by the last filming session for the show I'm currently working on, so I have plenty of time to grab a bite.

"No, Drew. You can't break my heart like that." Mum leans toward the dramatic. It's one of the things I love about her, since it makes figuring out what she's thinking easy. "You can't move to the other side of the world where I'll never see you again."

My laugh comes out fast and loud. "Laying it on a little thick, don't you think?"

"Drew." She draws out my name, but I hear the smile in her voice.

"You knew this was coming, that I was searching. If I had found it in Australia, then great, but I haven't."

The moment I drove the rental van into Seward, something sparked in my chest and all my muscles relaxed, like my body recognized home. I've traveled the world more than most, seen lots of beautiful places while filming my television show for the Nature Channel. Never have I reacted to a place like I did to this small Alaskan community.

"Mum, you're going to love it here. Mountains that jut up to the sky straight from the sea. All kinds of artists and little shops that sell local pieces." It's probably not fair for me to bring that up, but her passion can be used to my advantage, right?

"Bub, you are the smartest person I know, but right now you're a galah if you think I'll come where the houses are igloos and polar bears roam free." Mum makes a *tsking* sound like I'm off my rocker.

I just shake my head and laugh. "It's not like that. Alaskans live in houses just like everyone else, and the polar bears are hundreds of miles away. That's like saying all Ozzies have pet roos and wrestle crocs."

"Don't we though?"

"Mum." Now, I'm drawing out her name.

"This wouldn't have anything to do with a sheila would it?"

Mum's question pops Denali Wilde, one of the owners of North STAR Kennel, and my latest show assignment, to mind. I can't deny that part of the appeal of Seward is a certain, snippy dog trainer with dark, brown eyes I could get lost in and perfectly styled hair that makes me want to mess it up. But my heart had been set on this place the moment we drove in. Having a cute, serious neighbor would just be icing on top of the cake.

My phone beeps in my ear, signaling an incoming call. I glance at it. Seeing my producer's name, I tingle all over like I bathed in the icy bay.

"Mum, Steve's calling. I got to go. I'll send you pics."

"Won't change my mind." She sighs like it's the end of the world. "Love you. Stay safe."

"Love you too. Talk soon." I hang up, shifting my brain to the conversation I've been waiting all day for. "Steve, thanks for calling back."

"Well, when you said you have an idea for another show, I had to see what you had in mind." He chuckles, but it's a calculated sound. "When my top watched star who swears he's retiring calls, my interest is piqued."

After working for Steve for the last seven years, I've

grown to like him. Well, maybe like is too strong of a word. Let's say, I understand the bloke. He's all about what will make the network, and therefore him, money. Me being his most profitable asset the last seven years makes my position a balancing act. I have a certain amount of influence with him, but that influence comes with a price. How do I get what I want from the network without falling headfirst back into the thick of it?

"We're filming the last segment with the kennel this afternoon. I think you'll like what we've got." I'm skirting the edge of why I called him. I want to dangle some bait like all these Alaskan fishermen do before I set the hook.

I agreed to this special, highlighting interesting people working with animals, as an appeasement to me not renewing my contract. *Going Wild with Drew Wilder* is a thing of the past. Something only to be viewed in reruns, which knowing the way the network schedules things, the show has at least another ten years of airtime on those initial fourteen seasons I invested my time into. Seward and the women of North STAR Kennel are the last people I'm highlighting for the special, then I'm free.

Unless what I'm about to suggest happens.

Do I really want to get wrapped into a new show when I just got free of the last?

"Good. What you've sent over of the other organizations is stellar. This special is award-winning material, and we haven't even finished yet." Steve's getting excited, like he's had one too many of those fancy espressos his secretary makes him. "What about the girls? Are they as hot as their pics on their website? The episode will get even more viewings if we can highlight that along with what they are doing."

And then there's the Steve I can barely stand. The smarmy drongo that is more focused on monetizing people rather than producing great shows that not only educate but inspire. If it wasn't for *this* version of Steve, I might be tempted to keep my show running. I love traveling the world, finding wild animals not many have seen. Plus, the money has allowed me to volunteer my off time to different animal clinics around the world that are short on help. But the last year or so, filming has become a thing that drags me down instead of excites me. Suddenly, I'm not so sure about my proposal.

"They're incredibly smart and have something really special here," I answer, surprised at the guarded tone in my voice.

"Right. Smart." He draws out the words, and I swear if I could see him, he'd probably wink. "Now about your idea, kick it to me. I'm ready to field it." Steve thinks he's so cool, but he's constantly mixing sports jargon in his attempt to prove he's just one of the guys.

"I actually think there might be more here with these ladies than just an episode smacked in the middle of a special." I pace to the other side of the one-room cottage and glance at my notes scribbled on my paper. "What they are doing is exciting, and with the craze over anything Alaska, I think there might be a winner here."

"All right. What do you have in mind, mate?" His use of Aussie slang makes me cringe more than his misuse of sport references.

"Well, I say we follow them. Set up three or four weeks of filming their training sessions and calls out for search and rescue. I can be the bloke chatting with them, kind of like they are training me along with their dogs." I take a deep breath and plunge forward. "Between what the ladies are doing here, the Alaskan appeal, and me being a part of it, the show has great potential."

Now my skin is feeling oily, like I'm the smarmy one. But if I'm going to get Steve to even consider this, I have to sell it hard like a used car salesman.

Since meeting the Wilde cousins, I've wanted to find a way to help bring light to their project. They're such a diverse group of women struggling to start a breeding and training center that could revolutionize the way service dogs are trained. The fact that I overheard them talking about finances, or more like their lack of finances, put an entirely new level to my desire to help. They're the type of people who aren't going to take a handout, so I couldn't just give them the money they need. What better way than to have a TV show centered around them?

"So, we have hot girls, Alaska, and you? We can't go wrong! What's their last name again?" His question gives me pause, like I know what his reaction will be when I tell him.

I clear my throat, not wanting to tell him. "Wilde."

"You're kidding me? Wilde and Wilder?" Steve laughs so loud I yank the phone from my ear. It's not that funny. "I can see it now. The wild women of Alaska, taming feral dogs and men's hearts around the world." Steve's enthusiasm makes my skin crawl. "Have you talked to them yet? Think they'll go for it?"

"Not if you title it that, they won't." I try to keep my annoyance out of my voice. I'm not sure I'm successful so I blaze on. "But, if we highlight what they are doing rather than their looks, I think I can convince them to at least consider it. You'd have to make it worth their while, though. They aren't going to venture into this without a reason. They're busy, and adding a film crew and the hassle that comes with the extra people won't be something they'll jump on just for the sake of being on TV."

"So, they're money hungry?"

"Far from. They're driven, determined to make their kennel a success to help out others." I don't want Steve to get the wrong idea about the Wilde family. They won't do this series to gain fame or get rich. I can see it being a means to an end. An avenue to highlight the way service dogs are trained and the dedication that goes into that. "They'll be bringing something that hasn't been done before with Nature. It's tapping into the *Dog Whisperer* fame but with a level of adventure thrown in. You know that if you want to edge out the competition, you have to be willing to invest. I think these ladies are an investment that will pay back in large dividends."

I close my trap, letting my words settle. This opportunity could be just what they need to tip their business into success. Television was my means to an end to get my dreams, though I stayed far longer than necessary. Lost sight of what's important. Now, though, I'm back on track, and I'll be here to help the Wilde gang wade through this and not make my mistakes.

"Okay. I'll pitch it. Send me over what video you have of them so far." Steve chuckles low. "Anything that keeps the Midas touch going, I'm all over it like a chunky kid on a cupcake."

A bitter taste coats my mouth, and I sneer.

Okay, I lied.

I haven't grown to like him.

I hate the man.

Hate that he refers to me as his golden calf and that he's willing to sacrifice anything to bring in more money. Hate that I'm even thinking of suggesting a show to the ladies and furthering my need to work with him. But Nature Channel, as a whole, isn't a reflection of Steve's sliminess. If I can just minimize their exposure to him, be their middleman, they won't be subjected to this bugger.

I'm ready to end this call and bathe in hand sanitizer. "Well, I gotta go. I'll send you what I have. You let me know what the higher ups say."

"Will do, mate."

I hang up and toss the phone on the bed. Shoving my hands through my hair, I stomp back to the window as all kinds of doubts swirl in my brain. Is this really the best way to get the Wilde's the funds they need? Wouldn't it just be easier to loan them the money?

I shake my head and stare out the window at the calm water. Yes, but from the way Aurora and Denali had argued about borrowing more money, I can tell this is the option they'll take. Hopefully, my "golden touch" can rub off on them.

Chapter Two

-Denali-

I suck down the last of my cinnamon latte from the Rez coffee house to wash down their amazing cinnamon roll as I rush into the kennel. I may have an addiction to the spice, but I figure the medicinal benefits have to outweigh the sugar and butter content of the drink and pastry.

Right?

Probably not, but if I keep telling myself that, I don't have to worry about my daily stop at the shop.

Normally, I don't get the twenty-ounce latte, but I needed the extra encouragement for this afternoon. It'll probably keep me up way too late tonight, but Drew Wilder and the crew from the Nature Channel will be here any minute to shoot their last segment with my cousin Sadie.

Thankfully, I won't be anywhere near the cameras when they are shooting, but the crew makes me itch with nervous energy, like the time I rolled in a patch of poison ivy while visiting family in the lower forty-eight.

Okay, maybe not that bad, but I can feel the hives breaking out every time they come over for another session.

More like every time Drew comes over. Something about his wavy, dark blond hair and eyes so blue they resemble the ocean on a clear day has all my warning bells ringing. My clenching ovaries say it's attraction. I shut them down real fast.

It's not that, not that at all. I've done the whole superstar relationship thing before back in high school, and what did that get me? Nothing but a broken heart, crushed dreams, and a pile of responsibilities so high I'll never dig through them. I also have Sawyer, my eleven-year-old bundle of love, I'd fight to the death for like a rabid wolverine.

So, I can't complain.

At least, not out loud.

Without the mistakes of my past, I wouldn't have the love of my life. Doesn't mean I'm willing to go that route again over a sexy Aussie accent that slides warmth down my core faster than any latte ever could. Nope, I've locked down my heart one hundred percent against any and all twinges of attraction.

My cousin Sadie's troubled voice floats from the bathroom, so I venture down the hall to see what's bothering her in time to watch her lean into the small mirror. "You've got this."

Oh, this is too good. The charismatic Sadie is giving herself a pep talk. Glad I'm not the only Wilde who has to talk herself up to get through the day.

"Talking to yourself again?" I lean against the door-jamb and speak louder than normal for extra oomph, making Sadie jump and whack her head on the cupboard.

It's too much. I double over, the twenty ounces of latte sloshing in my belly as I laugh so hard I can't breathe.

"Ouch." She cringes, rubs the side of her head, and glares at me. "Not that funny."

"Are you kidding me?" I breathe in deeply to calm myself, wiping my finger under my watering eyes. Classic. I sigh. "I wish I'd caught that on video. We could have Violet put it on our YouTube channel under "Behind the Scenes" or something."

"Har. Har. Chuck it up, Buttercup." Sadie leans against the sink with her eyebrows pushed low over her eyes. The angry expression holds no weight since her lips keep jumping up at the corner like she's trying hard not to smile. "I don't remember you volunteering to be interviewed by the Nature Channel. If I remember right, your exact words were 'I'll be in front of the camera when penguins fly to Alaska and take up residence.'"

I mean it too. I have no desire to be in front of the camera. Sawyer already has one parent in the spotlight. He doesn't need another. Not that an episode on a nature show will suddenly make me a star. Or that Nathan, Sawyer's father and my ex, is obsessed with his status. He's just an amazing hockey player. Always has been. Still, the thought of getting in front of the camera makes me sick to my stomach and angry at the same time. It's a complicated mix of emotions I don't even understand.

Sadie cocks her head to the side and gives me a calculated look. Her wheels are spinning, and I'm pretty sure I'm not going to like what she's thinking. I need to get back to task and talk her up for this shot, not only so she'll rock it, which she will since she's a natural, but also so I move the attention off me.

"Guys, we have a problem." Aurora, my sister, rushes up behind me. Her normally pale skin is even paler, though I don't know how that's possible. "Reggie is sick."

Reggie is a beagle we took in last week to train. He has a lot of potential, and Sadie convinced her friend in Anchorage to let us work with him. We can't afford for a dog to get sick right now, not with how tight finances for the kennel already are.

Aurora holds the door open for Sadie and me, a look of horror on her face. Rory is the exact opposite of me in almost every way. While she loves the dogs and North STAR Kennel's mission, she's happy as a clam to just stay in the office crunching numbers or whatever it is she does all day behind the computer. We'd lose the business without her organizational and money skills. So, while she never would go on the outdoor adventures Sadie, her sister Violet, and I would dream up as children, I'm so thankful for Rory's complete opposite personality.

She steps up beside me and pushes her glasses higher on her nose. "What if it's parvo?" Rory whispers, glancing at the other dogs in the kennels like they might be able to understand her.

My heart flips in my chest like a bunch of salmon fighting to get up stream. If parvo, the devastating illness dogs sometimes get, passes through our dogs, the kennel tanks. All our adult dogs are vaccinated against it, but Sadie's wire-haired, pointing griffon female just had a litter of pups that aren't old enough to get the shot.

We could lose them all if it's parvo.

Then we'd lose the kennel.

My mouth feels like I've swallowed a bag full of cotton balls. I can't get words past the dryness.

"Mark's on his way." For not being too involved in the training, Rory loves animals and can't stand to see them sick.

It's a good thing the local vet is Rory's long-time friend. It doesn't hurt that he's had a major crush on Rory since high school. How she hasn't clued in is beyond me, but if Mark can't get up the nerve to tell her himself, I'm not going to tell her.

Sadie steps up to Reggie's enclosure to go in, but I snag her sleeve before she can open the latch.

"You can't go in there." I tug Sadie even farther away, like whatever he has might jump the five-feet distance and contaminate Sadie too. "The people from Nature will be here any minute. You can't go in there then handle the puppies."

Her gulp is so big it looks like it hurt. Reggie lays on the other side of the chain-link fence looking pathetic. All his pep has left him.

Sadie sighs. "I'll call Drew."

"No, you won't." I shake my head. Why would she even consider that? "The filming crew is leaving tomorrow. We can take care of this. You go do that interview."

"But—"

"No buts, Sadie." Rory pulls Sadie back toward the building, her quiet voice a contrast to my sharp, bossy one.

Sadie stares at Reggie for a few heartbeats, and I'm worried I'll have to push her more. Then, with a sharp nod of her head, she turns and marches toward the building. I sigh, then turn back to the kennels.

I'm not entirely sure what to do. I want to take Hank, my Belgium Malinois, from the kennel Rory put him in and rush him home where he'll be safe. If Reggie does have parvo, that could spread the heinous disease even further. Worrying over Hank is ridiculous. He's up on his shots, but the thought of him dying has my hands so sweaty they'd probably feel like a caught salmon. You know when the fish have sat in the cooler and gotten all slimy? Yeah. It's such an embarrassing side effect to my body freaking out. Always made holding hands real enjoyable.

Wiping my hands on my pants, I enter the gate and bend down to Reggie. "You under the weather, buddy?"

He lifts his head, and his tail thumps against the grass. It smells like an outhouse that hasn't been cleaned. I wrinkle my nose, hoping we can get the stink out when this is all over with.

Mark rushes up the side yard, his travel medical case slung on his shoulder. His gaze finds me with Reggie, then zeroes in on Rory like a heat-seeking missile. Her entire body relaxes when she sees him.

She puts her hand to her mouth and shakes her head. "I'm sorry to bother you, but I didn't know what to do."

"Hey. It's okay." He slides his hand along her shoulders and pulls her into a side hug.

She leans into him, putting her forehead on his collarbone. I just want to scream for them to get it together and hook up. I mean, they are perfect together. He's crazy for her, and I don't think going from friend to more would be a hard switch to flip in her brain.

"You did great. If it's parvo, keeping him here is the best." Mark gives her another squeeze, then sets his case down. "Let's see what's got Reggie down."

My phone buzzes in my pocket, making me jump as much as Sadie did earlier. Sawyer's bird call ringtone he set for himself chirps away, and Reggie tries to get up like he's ready to go hunting. I pull out the phone and squish the phone between my ear and shoulder, while I attempt to keep Reggie from getting up.

"What's up, bud?" The phone almost slips, so I crank my neck farther to the side and lift my shoulder up more.

"Mom, you'll never guess what I found!" Sawyer's excited yell has me jerking my head to the side.

The phone slips from its place and plops in the grass right next to Reggie's face. His eyes go all wide, and he lifts his head at me like I'm trying to decapitate him or something. I fumble with the phone, while I pet his head to calm him.

"What's that?" I'm half listening as Mark grabs a packet from his bag and steps into the kennel.

"I found a baby bird on my way home." Sawyer's my future vet.

Any injured animal has a home with him. We have so many homemade crates and cages in our back yard, it looks like a black market animal shopping center. Not that I know what one of those looks like. Seward, Alaska isn't exactly a hopping spot for stuff like that. I've tried to tell him he couldn't bring any more home, but I can't squash his passion. Besides, he's better at nursing the animals back to health than anyone I know.

Don't tell Mark I said that.

"Did you find the nest?" I ask as Mark lifts up Reggie's tail to swab for parvo.

The dog jolts up, bolting for the gate. My phone drops again, dangerously close to a splat of something nasty. I snag it from the grass and grab for Reggie's collar. Rory steps into the kennel and laces her fingers through Reggie's collar.

"Go ahead and talk with Sawyer. I'll help Mark." Rory tips her head toward the gate.

"Thanks." I'm up and out the gate. I'm about to put my phone to my ear when I remember the mystery ooze and think better of it. I click the phone to speaker, wishing I had a disinfecting wipe. Sawyer's still chatting away, not realizing I've been gone. "Sawyer, honey, I dropped you. I didn't hear anything you just said."

"Again?" The exasperation in his eleven-year-old voice makes me chuckle. "You need to duct tape it to your head or something."

"But then how would I beat you at *Spell with Me*?" We have serious competitions with the word game, even when he goes to stay with his dad. The kid beats me seven times out of ten, the stinker.

He snorts, and I love the sound. How I was blessed with the best dang kid around when everything else in my life is a mess is a mystery, but I'm not complaining. I'd be happy living in a shack in the wilderness if it meant I had him.

"So, this bird I found is pretty bad off. I think maybe another bird was trying to eat it or something." His voice is so filled with concern, it tugs at my heart. "I haven't figured out what it is yet."

"Do we need to take it in?" I squeeze my eyes shut

and pinch the bridge of my nose. I can't afford another vet bill, even if Mark gives me a steep discount.

Sure, I could dip into the savings I set up for Sawyer when he was a baby with the money Nathan sends, but I've never touched that. Not once.

"I don't know. I think I can help it, but I have to get it home first." Sawyer's voice is out of breath.

"Where are you?"

There's a pause. My heart rate goes into overdrive. He's a great kid, but he got the Wilde adventure spirit. I'm pretty sure he'll give me a heart attack someday.

"Lowell Creek waterfall."

Okay. That's not so bad. Except for the fact it's a favorite hangout of the local bears.

"Sawyer."

"Mom, it's okay. I brought the bear spray." His exasperation would be endearing if I didn't have images of bear maulings in my head. "And Lazarus."

Okay, the mutt Sawyer found and brought back from the brink of death would protect my baby from harm. Sweetest dog in the world until Sawyer is threatened. I once saw the dog chase off two dogs that had been terrorizing the neighborhood when they found their way to our yard. Even though Laz came back bloody and limping, those dogs left in worse shape.

"Where are you now?" I glance back at Mark and Rory who are talking quietly in the kennel.

"Almost home," Sawyer answers. "Mom, I think I can save this bird, but I might need your help."

This is the part about being a single parent that I hate. That feeling of being stretched so thin I'm transparent. I need to stay here and make sure Reggie is okay and that we don't need to do anything with the other dogs. I also need to be with my son, help him when he asks for it, because I know, at some point, he'll probably stop asking me.

How can I choose between my heart and our livelihood? Sawyer needs me, but Rory and Mark might need me here too. Especially since Sadie will be filming for who knows how long and Violet hasn't been seen all day.

These are the times I wouldn't mind having someone to share the load with. Being able to tag team would make life so much easier. That's not my reality, though, so I just need to suck it up and do the best I can with what I've got.

"Bud, listen. Reggie is sick." I hate that I'm letting Sawyer down. "I need to stay here for a while to see if Mark is going to need any help."

"What's wrong with him?" Of course, Sawyer would worry about the dog. He has a bleeding heart when it comes to animals.

"We're not sure yet. I'll be home as soon as I can. Is that okay?" I close my eyes and hold my breath.

"Mom, it's cool. Just do what you need to help Reggie. I'll be fine." His independence both hurts my mother's heart and makes me want to pump my fist in triumph.

I love that I can trust him, but I also know that one of these days he no longer will need me. Then where will that leave me? I swallow the loneliness that clumps in my throat.

"I'll be home as soon as possible." I'm surprised my voice doesn't sound all strained and emotional. Just goes to show I've become an expert at hiding my emotions. Like international spy level.

"Okay. Love you."

"Love you, too, buddy."

I tap the end call button and toss my phone on the table. I still need to disinfect the thing and don't want to risk forgetting and putting it up to my face. Marching across the yard, a list of what I need to do the rest of the afternoon starts forming in my brain. The quicker I can get through it, the faster I can get home to Sawyer. Hopefully, nothing else goes wrong.

Chapter Three

-*Drew*-

The filming couldn't have gone any better. Sadie is a natural in front of the camera, so laid back and friendly. Steve is going to eat her up the second he watches the segment. Not only did the filming go better than planned, but I got the distinct impression that Sadie wants me to go find a certain brown-eyed sheila.

Sadie's "While I clean up here, could you go check in with Denali for me?" had me cocking my head in confusion. I mean, why would she send me back there when both the vet and Rory were there? But the way Sadie wagged her eyebrows up and down and winked dramatically left little doubt that she was playing matchmaker.

I'm good with that, especially since I've been wanting to ask Denali out to dinner since the first time I saw her. Until I knew for sure that I was setting up shop here, there wasn't any reason to follow through with that desire. Seven years of traveling the world taught me that real quick. It took me a few tries, but after two difficult long-distance relationships, calling off dating until I settled seemed the smart move. Besides, dating only complicated my goals and divided my attention.

Now, though, my animal rescue center is within reach, so maybe looking past that goal to what the next step in life would be seems logical. Smart, actually. Heck, why not start my jump into the dating pool with the most beautiful and intriguing woman I've met in all my travels?

Just because it makes perfect sense in my head, doesn't mean it's an easy jump.

It's terrifying.

And exhilarating.

Especially since Denali has pretty much avoided me every time I've been here. That might be part of the appeal. A big part, actually. After being voted sexiest man alive by a certain popular magazine three years ago, celebrity life got even more crazy. You can't imagine the things some women do to get attention.

No one has ever accused me of being a tall poppy. I'm not conceited or overstuffed. I never wanted anywhere near that distinction.

One guess who pushed for that?

Yeah, Steve's a tosser.

Denali not caring a rip about my sexy status and ignoring me is so refreshing it's like I'm washed clean of all the griminess of the last three years. It also makes me wonder why, like lying awake at night for hours wondering. The only thing that has ever had me doing that is my rescue center.

In all that contemplation, I've come to the realization that I like things not handed to me. That's probably why all the propositions thrown at me lately have no appeal. My mum always said that something gotten easily isn't actually something I earned and usually wouldn't satisfy over time.

I learned that early on in life when my dear dad came around, showering me with gifts. He'd stay a day or two, drop tons of money on me, then disappear again. Eventually, he stopped coming altogether. Around five, I finally clued in. His stay didn't bring me joy. No, it only magnified the hole left by his leaving.

It might be slightly masochistic, but I like the idea of Denali not being particularly fond of me. Just to be clear, she's not rude or anything, just keeps her distance.

Starting today, I hope to close that distance one encounter at a time. Find out if there's something there or if it's all in my head. If I could spend seven years pocketing away money and doing a job that, though it was fun and exciting, had a lot of parts I didn't enjoy, I think I can take my time getting to know Denali. I'm all about patience.

I step into the back yard to find Denali scrubbing her phone with a wipe. This is no clean the surface job. The force of her rubs could take the picture printed on the case off. I smile at how adorable she looks with her face all scrunched up in concentration. A look of satisfaction widens her eyes as she lifts the phone close to her face to get a spot.

Boom! Heat explodes from my chest with such force I feel it all the way in my toes. I may be all about patience, but with this woman, eagerness might win over.

My feet use that heat as fuel to close the distance

between us. I shove my hands in my pockets to cool the jets and tone down my approach. I mean, I don't want to look like those fangirls I've been fighting off the last three years.

"How's Reggie?" I ask when I'm about a foot away.

She jumps and spins, dropping her phone in the grass and her arms swinging wide. The back of her hand knocks against my cheek with a loud *thwack* and has my ears ringing. She covers her mouth as her eyes go wide.

"I'm so sorry." She reaches for my face with a look of compassion but pulls back before she connects. "You startled me."

I shake my head and rub my cheek. "No wucka's. Don't worry about it. I didn't mean to sneak up on you." I grin with a chuckle. "I'll remember to make more noise next time."

Her eyes narrow a bit, and her arms cross over her body, her wariness returning. "You done with filming?"

"Yep. Sadie told me about the sick dog, so I wanted to see how he was doing." I tear my gaze from her and glance toward the kennel where the vet and Aurora Wilde converse. There's a beagle resting in the kennel, looking wrung out.

"Well, it's not parvo, thank God." Denali's stance relaxes as she sighs, and my attention is drawn back to her. "He probably just ate something that's upsetting his stomach. Mark injected Reg with fluids since he looked a little dehydrated, so hopefully by tomorrow he'll be himself."

"Good." I bend down to grab her phone and hand it to her as a text pops up. My nerves riot like a massive flock of cockatoos took up residence in my gut. "Listen, I was wondering if we could go for dinner, maybe grab some barbie or something?"

Her body tenses and eyebrows rise slightly. My heart pounds so hard in my chest I'm pretty sure she can hear it. She glances at her phone, then shoves it into her pocket.

"Sorry, I can't. My son found another orphaned animal, and I need to get home and help him." She lifts her hand in a stilted wave as she steps backward.

Several things are racing through my head, and I'm not sure which one to settle on. She has a son. Didn't know that. My eyes flick to her empty ring finger. That doesn't necessarily mean anything. Lots of people don't wear wedding rings, but, unless I completely misread Sadie's cues, Denali isn't in a relationship now.

Do I want to pursue something with a single mother? My own mum is amazing, but after my dad left, she could never quite trust again. Even botched a loving relationship with Vic, the only father-figure I ever had. Despite her breaking his heart, Vic stayed a constant in my life. Still is my closest mate, the one I think of as Dad. What if I end up like him with my heart ripped out but an attachment to Denali's kid?

Before I can answer that, I'm talking like my mouth has taken over the show. "I could grab a pizza and come look over the animal."

The left side of her face scrunches in doubt, so I quickly state my case. "You might not know this, but I'm actually a pretty decent vet. I have experience around the world and have volunteered hours in clinics with all kinds of animals."

Okay, mate. Shut your trap!

I clamp my mouth closed and rock back on my heels. She looks down then, over at her sister, before returning her gaze to me. Words bottle up in my mouth, but I push my tongue to the roof of my mouth to keep them in.

"Okay." Her agreement shocks me so much I swear my eyes bulge out of my head.

"What's yous favorite pizza?"

"Yous?" Her lips move toward a smile for the first time in my presence.

It's a small move, almost unnoticeable, but it makes that flock of cockatoos still hanging out in my core take off into flight as one, huge, fluttering mass.

"Aussie term." I shrug. "I may have spent the last seven years traveling the globe, but I'm still True Blue."

She gives a little *humph*. "Sawyer likes the Miner's Combo from the Klondike Pizzeria."

"And you?" I know I'm pushing, but if Denali is anything like my mum, she puts all her wants aside for her son.

She tips her head with a slight lift of her shoulder. "The Miner is good."

"All right." I won't push. Don't want her changing her mind on me now that I have my foot in the door. "Text me your address, I'll grab the tucker, and be right there."

"Tucker?" She makes a sound like an airy laugh, and I now plan on using my Aussie slang to my advantage.

"Food." I smile down at her, but she just rolls her eyes.

"Hey, Drew." Rory crosses the yard with the man, pushing her glasses up on her nose. "You done?"

"Yep. Your cousin was bloody brilliant." Steal the show brilliant. There's no way the network won't go for my idea. I point my chin toward the kennel. "Glad to hear the dog isn't too crook."

"He just scavenged the wrong thing to eat." The vet shrugs, then extends his hand. "Mark Fisher."

"Drew Wilder, nice to meet you." I clamp my hand in his. His grip is firm, and I like him already.

"I read your paper on effective rural veterinary set ups in the Outback, how you worked with that clinic to mobilize their services, including surgery. I'm using the info to set up my own mobile clinic." Mark adjusts his case on his shoulder.

"That's really sick, mate." I love hearing how my research and work with clinics help others. "I'd love to check it out sometime."

Denali's been typing on her phone while we talk, but my last comment has her head snapping up and her eyebrows V-ing over her eyes.

"That'd be great. Just swing by the clinic, and I'll show you the set up." Mark steps toward the building. "I'm going to peek at the litter before I head out. It was nice meeting you, Drew."

That's what I love about Alaska. No one cares a lick if you're a celebrity. Mark didn't talk about the show but about what I'd done in real life. Not that the show was fake or anything. I'm proud of what the show was, but I'm even more proud of the work I've done off-screen for animals.

"I'm heading out too." Rory extends her hand to me. "Thanks again for including us in your special."

"Nah, thank you for letting us see what you've got here." I take in the tidy kennels, big yard with different training areas set up, and the back of the building brightly painted with a massive mural of dogs and Seward's landscape, complete with four mermaids watching from the rocks in the ocean that look an awful lot like the Wilde women. "This facility and your program are amazing. It'll be fun to see how it grows."

"It is, isn't it?" Rory's smile is blinding as she gives Denali a side hug. "See you tomorrow, sis. Remind my main man I'll be by to pick him up for our weekly breakfast at the Rez at eight-thirty."

"Will do." Denali turns to me with her phone poised for typing as her sister walks away. "What's your number?"

"Here." I reach for her phone, and she hands it to me.

I type in my info, then I click on the contact info spot for a pic, lift up the phone, and snap a selfie. The look on my face is flat out ridiculous. I have a goofy smile that stretches practically from ear to ear, like I just saw a baby otter or something, and I want to delete the picture and take another one. The only reason I leave it is because taking another would make me look like a figjam.

"I'll just get going and grab that pizza." I hand her phone back to her. "Let me know where to deliver it."

"Okay." She scowls at her phone and shakes her head.

"Catch you later." I wave over my shoulder as I head to the building.

Sure, the phrase is just an Aussie way of saying goodbye. However, I can't help thinking I liked to take the literal definition of the words. Doubt about her son and whether she is unable to trust like my mum wheedle through the satisfaction. I'll just have to take things slow and reel up that patience I've mastered over the last seven years.

Chapter Four

-Denali-

What was I thinking agreeing to let Drew come over? Oh, yeah. I was seeing another vet bill being put on hold. I open the front door to the home Sawyer and I share with Sadie and toss my keys on the cluttered entry table. Glancing around the open room, I cringe at the mess. It's not pigsty disgusting, but it definitely isn't guest ready.

Books and magazines are strewn across the coffee table. My paperwork from the night before still waits for me at the breakfast nook. Sawyer's stack of crates and cages of various sizes line the far wall haphazardly like a bad game of *Tetris*.

Maybe if I rush, I can do the whole grab-and-stash clean? I'll just toss everything on my bed and take care of it after Drew leaves. He won't be seeing the inside of my bedroom door—ever—so throwing things in there real quick should take care of the worst of it. But then I won't be able to sleep until it's all put away.

"Ugh." I tip my head back and close my eyes. "This is why I don't entertain."

Why do I even care what the house looks like? It's not like he'll ever see the place again. He's leaving for who knows where tomorrow as he continues his trot around the world. That's it. I'm not going to worry that the dishes are piled in the sink and that I can see dust on the bookshelves.

Sawyer comes down the stairs with a bundle in his arms. His face lights up when he finally looks up and sees me. I love this kid with his short-cut, chestnut hair and big, brown eyes with lashes most women would kill for. Love the freckles that pop out across his nose and forehead when the midnight sun graces us again. Absolutely adore his quiet soul.

He may be shy around other people and prefer to be with his animals, but around family, he's a passionate kid racing toward adulthood. I can't believe he's already eleven. It seems like only yesterday I was a scared teenage single mom right out of high school, snuggling this precious bundle. My life's goals and dreams changed the minute this kid was placed in my arms. Nothing mattered anymore but him. He's still the reason for everything I do.

"Mom, you have to see this." He takes careful steps over to me, though I can tell by the joy radiating from his face he wants to run.

"What have you got this time?"

I've lost track of how many animals Sawyer has rescued. He's had porcupines, squirrels, dogs, cats, foxes, several varieties of birds. He even had a baby otter for a day before I found out and had him take it to the Sea Life Center. Each animal gets nursed back to health.

Most get released back to the wild when they are healthy.

Some stay members of our hodge-podge family. Hope, the fox with three legs and one eye, plays right alongside Lazarus, fetching balls and wrestling with Sawyer. People say I'm crazy for letting Sawyer do what he does and have a mini-zoo in our back yard. I might be, but I'm not about to squash this love and passion that's so strong in him.

Sawyer stops next to me, and I give him a side hug before turning my attention to his newest friend. Pulling back the soft fabric, I study the baby bird Sawyer has cradled in a blanket wrapped around a hot water pad. It looks weak and two shakes of its feathers away from death's door.

"Oh, Sawyer, it's so small."

I'm suddenly praying with all my might that Drew can help Sawyer save the small chick. My son may have a firm understanding that he can't save all the animals he brings in. Some are just too injured. That doesn't mean his tender heart doesn't take a beating when he loses one. He's so full of compassion and empathy, always has been since he was a toddler.

"I know." His hushed voice and crinkled brow tears at my heart. "I think I found her before it's too late, though."

He looks up at me with expectant eyes. I hope he did, because I can see his heart is already in love. I smile and give him another squeeze.

"I'm sure you did. I was messing with a sick dog this afternoon, so I'm going to go change real fast." I step away and head for my room. "We have company coming in a few."

"Okay."

He's so engrossed with the bird, I don't even think he hears me. Otherwise, he'd be peppering me with questions about the dog. His head snaps up from looking at the bundle.

"Wait. How is Reggie?" He stares at me with wide eyes.

"He had a rough afternoon, but he's going to be fine."

"Oh, good." He sighs and sits on the couch.

I rush into my bedroom, determined to change my clothes at least. The house can stay a mess. I, however, need out of this outfit. Who knows what I may have gotten in to while dealing with Reggie?

I strip off my T-shirt, toss it into the dirty clothes basket, and open my dresser. My phone rings, and I quickly snag the closest shirt. I pull it over my head and answer the call.

"Hello?" My arm gets caught in the body of the shirt, so I'm doing a sort of contorted dance trying to hear the caller and not look like I'm a two-year-old trying to dress herself.

"Hey, Denali. How's it shaking?" Nathan Blaine, Sawyer's dad, always starts our conversations this way.

I roll my eyes and shove my arm through the sleeve hole with an *oomph*. "To the right and kind of slow."

I never tell him how I actually am. It's been our routine since we dated in high school. As far as exes go, Nathan and I have a great relationship. Sure, he was part of my rebellious phase that ended with me pregnant. I had been such a dork growing up and couldn't believe the star hockey player was interested in me. There were a lot of things I regretted about our relationship and my willingness to set my beliefs aside. One thing I've never regretted is Sawyer.

Nathan and I knew that though we liked each other, we just didn't love each other. Neither of us wanted to be stuck in a marriage we didn't long to be in. So, after he was drafted to the pro-hockey team in New York straight out of high school, he stuck with his plan of going pro, working his way to better teams and coming home to Seward during his off-season to be with Sawyer. I cancelled my fall classes at the university, took up more hours at the vet where I'd worked all through high school, and tried to not let bitterness set in.

I'm not going to lie. It was hard at first. It took several years to realize that I didn't miss out on life because of having to raise Sawyer. He was the life I always wanted. Even without schooling, I still got my dreams of starting the kennel with the girls, but I also got to be the mom of the most amazing kid I know.

"Listen, I have some news. It's good, I think. I'm still processing, so I'm pretty sure it's good. Ugh. I don't know." Nathan rambles on, which is so not like him.

"Are you going to tell me or just mumble and grunt?" I jerk out of my jeans and grab a pair of leggings.

Some days I wish it would've worked out between us. He's a really great guy and a wonderful dad to Sawyer, even though he doesn't get to be here with him all the time. We had too many differences to make it work long-term and stifling his brilliance on the ice would've been tragic. I've never seen someone play with such genius and grace as Nathan does.

"Right. So, I got traded … to Colorado." He sucks in a breath and doesn't let it out.

"Nathan, that's a top tier team, isn't it?" I glance in the mirror and cringe at my shirt where Cookie Monster shoves a cookie in his face and the words "Me want more cookies" under him. The O's are chocolate chip cookies.

"Yeah. It's one of the best. The contract is"—he pauses for so long I wonder if I need to prompt him again—"it's huge, Denali. Like, stupid huge. I'm still in shock over it all."

"Nathan, that's great! You've worked so hard for this." I shrug at my reflection. Drew will get the entire at-home Denali tonight. I'm not changing again. "So, what happens now?"

"That's the thing I'm not so sure about." Nathan sighs. "I'll have to move to Denver immediately. They want me there for summer training, and I won't be able to come home."

"Oh." I slump on to the bed.

The summer is the only time Sawyer really gets to see his dad for a long stretch of time. This will crush Sawyer. I stare at the wall and try to think of how I'm going to soften this let down for my tenderhearted son.

"I know. I'm sick over it." A loud thump sounds over the phone, like Nathan hits a wall or something. "I tried to talk my way out of it, but management won't give. I either take their terms or walk. This position is life changing, but I don't want to hurt Sawyer."

"Oh, Nathan." I lean over and rub my fingers over my forehead.

"I know. I know. I hate this." He growls. "I need to be with him. Need our summer time together. Talking over video chat just isn't the same. Maybe … maybe he can come to Colorado for the summer and live here with me?"

My heart just stops dead in my chest. I'm suffocating, though I'm pretty sure my lungs still work. I always knew this might happen, but so far Nathan hasn't pushed to take Sawyer with him when he leaves for the season. I'm not sure I can handle Sawyer not being here, but it's also not fair of me to say no.

"I guess ... I guess you'll have to ask Sawyer what he thinks." Maybe it's the chicken's way out, but I can't give a cheery agreement.

There's a long pause in the conversation. The silence builds in my chest like an orca has snagged my leg and is pulling me into the deep, dark of the ocean floor. It's cold and dreary, a foretelling of what life without Sawyer here every day would be like.

Nathan's anguished sigh breaks my heart. "Sawyer will hate it. I can't make him leave his animals, leave you." His words have warmth returning to my limbs. "I'll have to figure something out, even if it means I fly back and forth on off days."

"We'll figure it out, Nathan. Sawyer will understand. He might not like you not being here, but he wants you to succeed more than I think even you want to." I wipe my face of tears I hadn't even realized had wet my cheeks.

"How did we get such an amazing kid?"

"I have no clue." My laugh comes out melancholy. "Nothing we did, that's for sure."

"Oh, man. You could say that again." He huffs, exhaustion thick in the sound. "I'll look at the schedule and come up with a plan before I call to tell Sawyer."

"Okay." I stand as a knock sounds at the front door

and Lazarus and Hank bark the alarm. "I'm really proud of you, Nathan. Really. This is an awesome break."

"Thanks, Denali. I'll talk to you soon."

We hang up, and I twist the phone in my hand. How am I going to cushion this blow for Sawyer? What I told Nathan was right. Sawyer will be excited for Nathan being traded. Doesn't mean my son's gentle heart won't be bruised, though.

Chapter Five

-*DREW*-

Okay. Patience is firmly back in place. It took the drive to the pizzeria, the twenty or so minutes it took to bake dinner, and the ten-minute drive to Denali's house to put it there, but I'm more than ready to just take things slow now. Now that a kid's in the mix, I can't just dive in. It's not fair to him if things don't work between Denali and me.

Keeping things as friendly as possible is key now. Kind of like wading into the ocean from the roped-off area instead of scaling the cliffs and back-flipping off the edge. While it's not as exhilarating, there's less likelihood of crashing on the rocks below or landing in a pod of angry sharks.

I glance at the cute two-story house where Denali's SUV is parked. A kid's bike lays on its side in the yard. The sky-blue paint is faded and the white trim peels in some spots. Despite that, the grass is cut short and perennial flowers spring from their beds in bright, colorful glory. A porch swing with bright pillows hangs on the porch, waiting for people to sit and chat. It's a house with character. A home that invites one to come and visit, maybe stay for a while.

It's like a siren's call to me, luring me in.

I shake off the feeling and push the door open. Can't have Denali catching me staring at her house like some creeper. Grabbing the pizzas, I make my way to the door. My knock is greeted with two dogs barking, instantly making me feel even more at ease.

The door opens, and I'm staring at Denali's son. He looks like her with his big, brown eyes, dark, red hair, and small, upturned nose. His eyes widen and mouth starts flapping like a snagged salmon just pulled up to shore.

"Hi, I'm—"

"Drew Wilder?" The kid cuts me off. "*The* Drew Wilder is at my door?"

I chuckle and lift the pizzas. "Yep, and I brought grub."

His gaze flicks down to the pizza then back up to my face. "You've got to be kidding me!" A big dog that looks part Rottweiler, part wolf barks at the kid's back and tries to push forward. "No, Laz. He's a friend." The kid pushes the dog's massive head behind him and turns back to me. "What are you doing here? I mean, Mom said you were coming to interview Sadie, but there probably wouldn't be time for you to do much else."

Denali hadn't wanted me to meet her kid? I'm not sure how that makes me feel. Defensive? Yeah. It's not like I'm a jerk or some conceited superstar or anything. Understanding? Definitely. If she's half as protective as my own mum was, she probably didn't want to risk her son getting hurt. Plus, Denali hasn't been the warmest, so there's that.

"Well, my schedule opened up." I shrug. "Plus, your mum said you had an animal that needed looked at."

"Oh, this is great." He turns and looks over his shoulder as he walks into the living room. "I saw how you helped that kakapo in season three, episode eight. You can definitely help out this little one."

My step falters as I'm now gaping at the kid. I don't even know the seasons, let alone episode numbers of when I helped certain animals. Sure, I know the handful of my favorites, but I'm the one who filmed them.

"Or that time you helped that cassowary chick. I thought the mom was gonna peck your eyeballs out." He turns around with a smile, like my almost-blinding was epic. This kid is a superfan if I've ever seen one, which makes me even more curious why Denali didn't let him meet me earlier.

"I'm Sawyer, by the way, and that lug is Lazarus." Sawyer points to the massive dog sniffing my leg as I walk. "You've probably already met Hank, which makes sense. He normally isn't this laid back when people knock."

Hank lays in a dog bed in the corner of the room with a fox curled up next to him. It's built up like a small, blue throne with his name painted on the front. There's a matching one in red with Lazarus's name on it. On the other side of the room are two more with Coco and Rowdy, Sadie Wilde's two dogs' names. The rest of the wall space is taken up by bookshelves and various sizes of animal crates, all stacked haphazardly.

This family is something else. A warmth sparks inside my chest. It feels, I don't know, like kinship. Like

I've finally found others like me. It feels an awful lot like I'm finally home, and I'm snatching at my patience as it tries to float away like a helium balloon.

Sawyer leads me to the dining room and kitchen and leans over a box on the table. I set the pizzas on the counter and join him. A small, white fluff of feathers nestles among soft fabric. Its head turns up and black eyes stare up at us from a gray mask of feathers.

"Sawyer, do you know what this is?" My voice is an awed whisper.

"Well, I know it's a bird of prey from the hooked beak, but I haven't wanted to leave it to check my reference book." Sawyer's forehead scrunches as he gently runs the back of his finger along the chick's side. "It could be a bald eagle or maybe a golden. There are a lot of those around."

"Nah, mate. This here is a peregrine falcon." I point to the black feathers along the bottom of the wing. "See those dorsal feathers on the wings?" I continue after Sawyer nods. "That's only found on the falcon."

"But that doesn't make sense." Sawyer's head shakes. "I didn't find this guy near the cliffs."

"Sometimes falcons nest outside the cliffs. It's rare but does happen." I lean closer to the box. "Could be that another bird snatched the little bugger from its nest and dropped it."

"That makes sense." Sawyer carefully scoops the chick up. "It's scraped up on the side. See?"

He holds the bird so I can see the side. There's a gash along the body under the wing. It's not too deep, and Sawyer has already cleaned it well.

"You did a good job there, doctor." I smile at him

with a nod. "She'll heal up nicely if you can keep her fed and warm."

"I have baby bird food I made from earth worms, crickets, and soaked cat food that I blended then froze from the last bird I found." Sawyer nods his head toward a vacuum-sealed packet thawing in a plastic container on the counter.

I love this kid. Can't help it. He's not only me on steroids when I was growing up, but his concern is so genuine and overpowering.

"What did your mum think of you putting worms in her blender?" I can't keep the laughter out of my voice.

"Oh, I used my own blender." Sawyer cringes. "Actually, it was hers until I blended mice in it for the fox kit I was nursing."

"You put mice in her blender?" I choke on my spit as I suck in a gasp. I was wrong. He's on a totally different level than I ever was.

"Yeah." His eyes sparkle as he looks at me. "You should've seen the look on her face when she walked into the kitchen just as I dropped the mouse in."

"Did she shriek and throw a fit?" I can imagine my mum doing that. Or faint. She totally would've fainted.

"Nope. Just turned around and left the house." Sawyer's love for his mom shines through in his voice. It was laced with respect and a bit of awe. "Twenty minutes later she came back home with a new blender. Said I could keep the other one."

"Wow. My mum would've lost it." My admiration for Denali rises even more. "Your mum is pretty special."

"No, she's more than special. She's the best."

Sawyer's declaration is final, and I'm thinking he might just be right.

"Hey, you two. Have you figured out what you found yet?" Denali's twisting her red hair into a messy bun as she walks into the kitchen.

She's wearing the most ridiculous shirt but somehow still looks amazing in it. Her eyes are pink and shiny, like she's been crying. I want to ask if everything is okay, but remember I'm supposed to take it easy. Every minute I spend talking with her son and hearing more about her makes my tenuous hold on my patience weaker and weaker.

"Drew thinks it's a peregrine falcon. How cool would that be?" Sawyer sets the bird back in the box, and I'm glad his initial shock of seeing me has faded to acting like I'm just a friend.

"That would be super cool." Denali peeks in the top pizza box, then raises an eyebrow at me. "You realize there's only three of us, right?"

"Yeah, well, I'm hungry." I shrug and am slightly thrilled the piece she grabs is one of the pineapple and ham I ordered.

"Mmm. I think Klondike must make the best pizza in the world." She closes her eyes as she chews her bite, then looks at me. "Thanks for dinner."

"You're welcome." I clear my throat and tear my eyes from Denali to Sawyer.

He's smiling as his gaze bounces back and forth between me and his mum. Oops. I have to do a better job at keeping the attraction for Denali stifled. The last thing I want is to hurt this awesome kid or make him expect more between Denali and me than there might end up being.

"You know, mate, you nurse this chick to adulthood, and you could train her for falconry." I go to the kitchen sink and wash my hands.

"Oh, man. That would be totally epic." Sawyer squeezes in next to me. "I've been wanting to do that forever. Even joined the Alaska Falconers Association and have been studying for the test. There's a falconer here in town that lets me come out with her. I never imagined I might actually get my own falcon so soon." He peeks out the window into the back yard, then turns to me. "Hey, would you like to see the rest of the animals I'm helping?"

Seriously, I need to stop right here and now. Just turn around and walk out the front door. I've never met a kid like this before, someone as passionate about animals as I am. If I'm not careful, I'm going to end up just like Vic, fully in love with not only the mum but the kid too, with no chance of a relationship.

Not that I'm in love with Denali. Deep attraction, yes, but not love. Sawyer? I'm already so enamored with this kid, there's little hope of me getting loose from his snare unscathed.

Chapter Six

-Denali-

I sit on the porch swing with a sigh and pull my knees up to my chest. Sawyer and Drew's voices float over the fence. Not words so much, but high-pitched excitement countered by low steadiness.

While I thought having Drew here would be awkward, it was the total opposite. His easy-going manner and way he talked to Sawyer had me relaxing my guard some ... too much maybe. I shift on the seat and lean my chin on my knees.

Plus, the dude got my favorite kind of pizza. Sawyer was quick to point that little nugget of information out. Drew's smile when he looked at me and declared it his favorite too shouldn't have had me going all melty like the cheese pulling from the pizza. It really shouldn't.

I mean, I dated America's hockey sweetheart. Heated looks should have no effect on me. Of course, that was eleven years ago, and I've been out of the dating game for a long ... very, very, long time.

I'm not even sure the handful of dates I've gone on

since Sawyer was born count. I went so my sister and cousins wouldn't feel bad for me but didn't really give the guys a chance. I'm happy being home with Sawyer, and dating is just so much work and time.

I have Sawyer to think of. How would the man I'm dating treat Sawyer? What if Sawyer gets attached but the relationship didn't work out? What if my son felt like I didn't love him anymore because my attention was divided? So many questions and things to consider that dating seemed like too much of a gamble.

Seeing Drew with Sawyer, watching through the kitchen window as the man really listened to what Sawyer had going on and gave tips and encouragement, that was too much for me to handle without the what-if's popping up. I mean, the two of them are so alike, what if I gave in to the attraction swirling beneath my skin, making goosebumps rise with Drew's warm glances and sexy accent?

That question had me racing to the front porch where the only thing I can watch is the occasional car passing by and the neighbor's cat chasing butterflies. It's dull enough it should have put my mind back on track. It's the track I've been firmly on the last eleven years. The track that keeps my son healthy and happy and the Wilde women's dreams of starting a kennel that will train dogs to help others chugging on toward success.

We are making it, despite the tight budgets. I've sacrificed so much to stay on course. I can't let a man that will be leaving have me jumping the rails and careening down the mountainside.

Plans ... that's what will keep my mind where it should be. I grab my phone from the table next to the swing and type out what I need to get done tomorrow.

Then I move on to what needs done this weekend. Thirty minutes later, I'm so deep in the list of improvements for the kennel I want to implement and a game plan to how to get that done without strapping our budget even more, the slap of the screen door shoots my head up so fast I might have whiplash.

"Sorry." Drew smiles, his dimples caving his cheeks in beneath the dark blond, evening stubble.

That one word slides along my skin, and I shiver. All that time I spent diverting my attention hasn't helped control my reaction to him. Good thing he's leaving tomorrow. I'm not sure there are enough plans in the world to distract me long-term, and that would end in disaster. Sawyer already has one father who isn't around much. Me getting involved with another man who made his living traveling the world would not only be hard on Sawyer, but would be wildly unfair.

"Thanks for coming and looking at the bird. It really means a lot to Sawyer." I want to show my appreciation and get the man moving on to his next great adventure. Then my skin can get back to behaving, and I can return to normal life without attractive TV stars bringing pizza to the house and wooing my son with stories.

"No worries." He sits down on the swing.

My skin breaks into goosebumps upon goosebumps with his nearness. I force myself not to scoot away. Maybe if I stay where I am, I'll train myself not to react. It works with conditioning dogs. Shouldn't it work with me too?

"Sawyer's amazing. Truly. He's a fair dinkum vet, better than a lot of blokes I've had to work with over the years." He leans back and crosses his ankle over his knee, making it press against mine.

My leggings suddenly feel too tight and itchy. I take a breath through my nose and leave my leg where it is. Can't condition myself if I pull away.

"He's dedicated, has been asking for veterinary books for years for his birthday and Christmas. The first year he asked, Nathan and I both got him kids' books on animals." I shake my head as the memory surfaces. "Sawyer isn't a spoiled kid, hardly ever asks for anything for himself. The look of disappointment on his face had both Nathan and me scrambling to make it right. The next week, he was engrossed with the Merck Veterinary Manual and Sounder Comprehensive Dictionary and the kids' books were donated to the library."

"Crikey! How old was he?" Drew leans away so he can look at me, and I stifle my laugh at his shock.

"Six," I answer with as straight of a face as I can.

"Six?" He sits back with a huff, his foot slipping off his knee and slapping the porch with a thud. "No wonder he spoke circles around me. At six, I was still picking my nose and wondering if Mum gave me Vegemite Snackabouts or Twisties in my lunchbox."

"Oh, he still did that too." I wonder what Drew looked like when he was six. I hope he was one of those awkward kids with too big ears and bad, mom haircuts. More than likely, he was the kid all the girls swooned over by the swings. "Though Sawyer probably wouldn't touch Vegemite with a ten-foot pole." I make a gagging face.

"What are you saying? That spread is the best." He crosses his arms when I cringe and shake my head. "Have you ever actually had Vegemite?"

"Yep. One of the summer employees for the wildlife tour went to our church when she was here. Had us all try it." I can almost taste the bitter, malty, non-jelly now. "Living in Alaska, I've eaten a lot of different foods, but that one takes the prize for worst."

"Nah, mate. You must not've eaten it right." Drew's shaking his head, his accent getting thicker. "Toast, a spread of heaven, and some slices of avocado and you got yourself a right, tasty meal."

"If you say so." Though wasting an expensive avocado and mixing it with that isn't what I would consider tasty ... or economical. I need to move the conversation on, get his accent back to normal sexy, instead of super-charged, Aussie sexy. "So, do you think the falcon will make it?"

"Yeah, I think she will." He leans back in the swing and gives it a little push. "Sawyer already had the beaut patched up as much as I could do and with his blender of nasties, the chick will be fat and happy before long."

I shudder at the thought of what Sawyer puts in that blender of his. My old blender. I try not to think about how many pet meals he made in that thing before I found out.

Drew laughs. "He told me about you catching him dangling a mouse over the blades."

"Talk about gagging." My face scrunches.

"He said you were chill." Drew stretches his arm across the back of the swing, and I pull my knees tighter to me.

He's not touching me, but I can sense the heat of him across my neck. It feels good, like something I've been missing. I tamp down the feeling. I'm not about to get twitterpated over someone who after tonight I'll never see.

"What he doesn't know is that halfway down the block I had to pull over and toss my cookies in the neighbor's irises." I roll my eyes. "I felt bad until the old biddy asked if I was pregnant again."

"Blimey. Who does that?"

"Right?" I stretch my toes to the floor and relax back into the sway of the swing. "She didn't even have reason to think that. I haven't dated anyone since Nathan, so her words were just plain rude."

"Nathan must be Sawyer's dad then?" Drew's voice holds curiosity.

"Yeah, my boyfriend senior year. The only time I ever rebelled against the rules."

"So, he was a bad boy?" Drew's chuckle sounds forced.

"No, the opposite, actually." I really don't want to get into this right now, but maybe if I tell him, he'll understand why I've kept my distance. "Nathan was the high school hockey star. Still is, a hockey star, I mean. He graduated high school and all, then went off to play in New York."

"Nathan? Nathan Blaine? Carolina's center who scored the most points ever in a single season?"

"You follow hockey?" I turn to him, shock clear in my voice.

"I have a lot of time stuck in hotel rooms by myself." He shrugs, but the comment makes my heart hurt a little. "I got hooked on hockey. And pickle ball but for totally different reasons."

"Hmm." I turn back forward as silence falls between us.

My thoughts keep spinning around Drew's interaction with Sawyer and the sense I get that he's lonely. I'm not sure what to say. The silence grows thick as we swing back and forth.

"Why didn't you want Sawyer to meet me?" Drew's question is low and laced with hurt.

I never meant that. I only wanted to protect Sawyer. That's all I think about, actually. So much so that I'm not even sure what not thinking each move I do through my Sawyer-tinted filter would feel like.

"A few years ago, another TV personality came through town doing a special at the Sea Life Center." I take a deep breath before I barrel on. "Sawyer was so excited, spent all the money he'd saved for some new crates to see the guy. The man gave him a pat on the head and brushed him off like he was nothing more than a barnacle."

"Let me guess. That was Eugene Little." Drew practically spits the name out.

"Yeah. That's the man." I lean my head back, and Drew's forearm flexes against my neck. "I wasn't about to let that happen again, not after how much it crushed Sawyer the first time."

"I get that." Drew gazes at me. He's so close his breath blows against my ear as he talks. "I want you to know I'd never do anything to hurt Sawyer."

Drew's words pull my eyes to his determined expression. He may think that he won't hurt Sawyer, but my son's heart is too big. Taking in this lonely Aussie hero would be far too easy for Sawyer. Far too easy for me, as well. Thank goodness Drew is leaving in the morning.

Chapter Seven

-*DREW*-

My hands slick with so much sweat, I'll probably find a puddle of salt water on the floorboard. When I got back to my hotel room after one of the best evenings I can remember, Steve called and gave me the go ahead. The big wigs love the footage for the special and the premise for a series and gave Steve the green light to move forward.

Which gives me the job of agent, so to speak.

Steve wanted to call them himself, but I slapped that thought down faster than a kook on a sick wave. With the first sentence from his lips, he would probably ruin everything. Since seeing Denali's finances sprawled across the kitchen table, it's even more necessary for this to work. Things are tight for her, which is surprising given Sawyer's dad is one of America's best hockey players ever ... that was a shocker tidbit of info. Hit a bit too close to home, though it seems like Nathan is a better dad than mine ever was.

I shake my head. I guess it's not all that surprising

Denali wouldn't ask Nathan for help, with the conversation I overheard. Denali was very adamant about not asking for handouts. That trait probably bleeds into her personal life too.

That's why I can't let Steve bugger this meeting up. It's also why I made Steve go back to the network for more money upfront, taking the additional out of my contract. If we are going to do this, it has to be a game-changer for the Wilde's.

I pull into an empty parking spot at the North STAR Kennel and let out a long breath. I just need to go in and barrel through this. If there are oppositions, I'll deal. If they shoot me down, that's okay too. At least I tried. In fact, that would mean I'd be free of the network now. A part of me hopes they'll say no, that I can finally cut ties completely and move on with life here in Seward.

Nope. I can't let that thought settle in too deep or I might not make the most compelling pitch. Pushing the door to the rental car open with determination, I rush to the building before I can change my mind.

The kennel doesn't have a normal bell that announces visitors. A howl sounds as I step across the threshold, reminding me that I need to ask them where they got that. I'd love to have something similar at the rehabilitation center.

The room is dark after the bright summer sun, so I snap off my sunnies and scan the room. My gaze lands on Sadie talking with a guy on the couch. Perfect. If I can get her excited, I might be able to pull this off.

"Drew, what are you doing here? I thought your flight was this morning." Sadie's forehead scrunches over her eyes.

"Sadie, I have the most amazing news." I cross to the couch and pull her up, nerves bubbling in my gut. Maybe I shouldn't have eaten breakfast. "Are the others here?"

"Sure, let me go get them." She turns to the man sitting on the couch. "I'll be right back."

I'm such a jerk, interrupting like I did.

"No worries. Take your time." The man waves her off, and she rushes out the room to the back.

"Sorry to interrupt, man." I outstretch my hand. "Drew Wilder."

"It's not a problem." His easy manner reflects his words. "Bjørn Rebel."

I'm about to ask Bjørn if he has a dog he's training when Sadie returns with her sister and cousins. My gaze takes them all in but settles on Denali. Nerves bounce off her as she wrings her hands in front of her. I need to chill, approach them with calm so she doesn't bolt. I relax my shoulders as I step toward them.

"Did the Nature Channel not like the interview?" Denali asks, a tightness in her voice.

"No. I mean, they loved it." I grab her hands in both of mine to still them, then drop them as heat races up my arms. I push through the sensation and turn to the others. "They want us to do an entire series."

"What?" Violet gasps, her hands going to her cheeks and excitement sparking from her eyes.

"What do you mean, series?" Denali crosses her arms over her chest, her eyes narrowing, which doesn't surprise me.

"Nature loves the idea of a group of amazing women defying odds and attacking the Alaskan wilderness head on." I point at the ladies, trying to contain the excitement in my voice but failing.

Aurora chuckles, while Denali rolls her eyes. Great, that's two nos. Sadie just stares, not saying a word, and a bead of sweat makes a long, cool trail down my spine. She chews on her index finger's knuckle, while her other hand holds her elbow. At least one of them isn't blowing me off.

"We aren't doing anything that every other woman and man in Alaska aren't doing as well." Denali shakes her head, and my opinion of her rises even more. "It's called life. It's no different from anywhere else."

"Sure, but viewers are obsessed with Alaska." I motion around the room with my hand at the beautiful kennel they remodeled themselves. "With you ladies being adventurous *and* gorgeous, people will jump on this like a wolf pack on a downed caribou."

"I'm not sure I enjoy being referred to as prey." Denali glares, and she pulls her arms tighter around her front like she needs to protect herself. "And I definitely don't want to be forced to stage things for some audience like a joke. I mean, there's not much *real* Alaska in those shows everyone is so obsessed with."

"We wouldn't film ours that way." I've got to fix this. What was I thinking, referring to them as caribou? "I'd make sure that everything we did was authentic. The last thing I'd want is to make you look bad or uncomfortable."

"Too late for that." Denali mutters low, but the words make me feel slick and slimy, like I got dipped in a vat of seal oil.

"How would this work exactly? What are you

wanting to film?" Sadie finally speaks, turning everyone's eyes to her.

Denali's mouth pops open like she can't believe that Sadie wants to consider the idea. Violet, on the other hand, bounces on her toes like a roo. Aurora is more pensive, just pushing her glasses up on her nose and cocking her head at Sadie.

"Me and two other cameramen would stick around for a month or two and film what you all do." I shrug like it was no big deal, but the tension in my shoulders gives me a headache. "Nature will pay a generous amount upfront, then you'll receive royalties when the show produces above and beyond that initial payment."

"Just film us throughout the day? How is that going to be TV worthy?" Sadie's voice is slightly incredulous, and if I don't play this right, I'll lose them. "It's not always hopping fun around here."

"That's all right. The mundane interests people as much as the wild." I shove my hands in my pockets, so I don't wave them wildly like a mad man.

"How much is generous?" Aurora crosses her arms, and in that moment, there is no denying she and Denali are sisters.

"I mean, you'll have to negotiate, which I suggest you do, but they are already prepared to offer six figures"—I count to three, then add—"each."

"But what would they film? It's not like what we do is all that exciting." Denali waves her arms around, and I can tell that her anxiety is building.

Violet wraps her arm around Denali's waist and squeezes. I hate that I'm making her uncomfortable. Maybe I should just call the entire thing off.

"Denali, I know you didn't want to be in front of the

camera, but this isn't something we can pass up." Sadie sighs. "Think about what we could do with the dogs, what we could do for the community. We wouldn't have to wait to expand."

"If we play it right, we could make even more on merchandising, not to mention the fact that the exposure could bring us more clients." Aurora's voice holds finality, like them doing it is a done deal, but Denali shakes her head.

"It could also backfire. We aren't that entertaining." She hugs herself tight again, and I want to punch myself in the face for even suggesting the show.

"There's plenty of room in the chopper for a camera or two." The low rumble of words from the couch pulls all our attention to Bjørn. "We were already planning training trips for your search and rescue dogs. If you filmed those first, you'd have time to figure out how you wanted to do the law enforcement side of the business."

I want to leap over the table and give the man a hug.

"That could work." Sadie turns to me. "Would the network pay for fuel?"

"Yep." I turn to Bjørn, a smile pushing my cheeks up and making them hurt.

Bjørn gives me a small shake of the head, reminding me I haven't sealed the deal. I can't get cocky.

"If Bjørn's a regular on the show, would he get paid for that as well?" Sadie crosses her arms, her face steely in a challenge.

I really can't wait to get to know this family better.

"Yeah." I haven't thought of those details, but I can work something out with Steve. "I don't know specifics, but usually others are paid for each second on air."

"So, if he's on the screen for ten minutes of an

episode, he'd be paid six hundred seconds?" Aurora asks, her teeth chewing on her bottom lip in concentration.

"That's right. I'm pretty sure."

"Will you help us make sure he gets a premium rate and that his business is showcased as well?" Sadie lifts her eyebrow at me, her eyes flicking to Denali.

She has her fingers pressed along her eyebrows while she shakes her head. Sadie baits me with my attraction to Denali. She knows it.

I know it.

Doesn't stop the lion bristling my hackles and making me want to roar in protection. Not just for Denali, either, but for this entire family. For the way they are protecting each other. For the way they think about extending the opportunity to their friends. I suddenly want this show to solidify my relationship with them, even if the only relationship that ever builds is friendship.

"I'll help however I can to make this the most beneficial to everyone." Maybe I put too much force in my words.

I don't regret it. Not with the way Denali finally looks at me, like she's counting on me to help. Like she wants to believe what I'm saying is true. I'm not sure how I'll pull it off, but I'll do whatever I can to earn her, all of their, trust.

Chapter Eight

-Denali-

"Sadie, Rory, please, we don't need to do this." I slam the cast-iron skillet down on the stove and flinch at the loud bang. I'm trying to wheedle our way back to sanity with rockfish tacos, black beans, and homemade salsa, but if I keep banging things around, I'm not going to get very far. "We'll make it without turning ourselves into a circus act."

"I really don't think that is what Drew is going for." Sadie sounds just like her mom when we used to try to talk our way out of mischief. "He wants to help us, Dee, not hurt. He promised he'd do everything he could to keep the show something we all will be proud of."

"And we're just going to accept his promise? We don't even know the guy!" I chop through the tomatoes with a bit too much force.

My knife more mashes them than dice. I scrape them into the bowl. It all tastes the same anyway.

"We might not know him all that well, but what we've done with him so far wasn't bad." Sadie reaches across the counter from her perch on the barstool and snags an orange sweet pepper slice. "My sessions for the special were a lot of fun."

She just doesn't get it. I don't want to have sessions. I don't want to be in front of the camera, worried if my crazy hair has popped out of its control or if I have a booger hanging out. I don't want something that will take up my time and pull me away from time spent with Sawyer, especially with Nathan's news that he won't be around. I just want to take care of my family and train superior dogs.

"Yeah, well, not all of us love the limelight." I motion between me and Rory, who is sitting next to Sadie, reading over the contract again. "Remember, this side of the Wilde family doesn't think we have to live up to our name. That's yours and Violet's job."

Rory's lips twitch up on one side as she pushes her turquoise glasses up on her nose. Sadie slumps back in her stool and crunches into the pepper. She can't refute my statement, not with how outgoing and adventurous she and Violet are.

My cousins constantly came up with new adventures for us to have growing up. Sadie is the driven one, not afraid to put herself out there to make big things happen. Violet is the eccentric artist who will jump from a plane just so she can get a different perspective for a painting. While Sadie is focused and Violet is, well, flighty, they both push things to the max while Rory and I either follow grumbling or watch from the side.

Me? I'm the grumbler, not wanting Sadie or Violet to have to go it alone. Rory? Yeah, after about fifth grade, she was happiest with her nose in a book, curled up on the couch. I envy her sometimes when taking care of everyone else starts to drag me down.

"Whatever. You did high school theater right alongside me." Sadie pops the rest of the pepper in her mouth.

"As a miscellaneous chorus girl, not the lead, remember?" I point the knife at her, then go back to chopping. "I spent more time working on the set than actually being on stage."

Sadie just rolls her eyes. Rory clears her throat and shifts in her seat. It's her sign that she's about to say something she doesn't want to. She's done it since we were little, mostly when we'd make her lie about going where we weren't supposed to be. Dread drops like a two-pound halibut fishing weight into my stomach.

"You and I might not be up for lapping it in the limelight, but I just don't think we can pass up this opportunity." Rory sets the contract on the counter and presses her palms to it.

"We're making it okay. We don't need this." I snatch an onion from the basket and slide the knife through it.

"Yeah, sure, we make ends meet but just barely." Rory shrugs one shoulder and glances between us. "Honestly, though, it's like we've tried stuffing a humpback into a swimsuit, and we're bulging at the seams."

Suddenly, I'm picturing a giant whale squeezing into a neon pink, polka dot one-piece. The stitching has pulled so much it looks like those trendy outfits where the sides are laced together instead of sewn. I laugh. Rory has a way with words, and I'm not liking the image of our budget she's created.

My hand stills, poised over the onion. Maybe if I don't move, the problem will leave, kind of like when you cross a bear on the hiking trail. Running and screaming only prompts it to chase, while staying calm and moving slowly usually has the bear passing on in indifference.

Unless of course it's a rogue bear. Then you better hope you're the fastest person in your group or are packing, maybe both. I feel like what Rory is building up to is as unavoidable as the rogue bear.

"There's just a lot of expenses we didn't consider." Rory sighs.

"But we crunched those numbers until I was dreaming dog food costs." I push the knife into the onion and peel the skin.

"We didn't expect to grow as fast as we have. It's awesome, but the income hasn't caught up yet."

I know this. Rory had mentioned it last week, but I didn't realize it was as bad as what she's saying. Tears sting my eyes. I'm glad I'm chopping the onion and can blame the vegetable for the sudden emotion.

"If you're dead set against this, we could ask for help." Sadie softens her voice and leans forward.

Rory sighs. "We won't qualify for a loan. I've already checked, so the only options we have are to ask Nathan to help out, dip into the money you've put aside for Sawyer, or do this show with Drew."

I'm shaking my head before Rory even finishes. They're all horrible options. I've made it a point to not ask Nathan for anything extra, not in all the eleven years since Sawyer was born. Don't get me wrong. Nathan's an amazing dad. Sends money every month for expenses, however, I've put every cent of that money away for Sawyer's future. Only my parents and the girls know.

To me, it doesn't exist.

It's untouchable.

Even when things are tight and my family not so subtly suggests I use it.

If Sawyer is going to have dreams, he's going to have funds to achieve them. Not that I want to spoil the kid, but because I don't want lack of money to stop him from achieving his potential. He's such a hard worker, so he wouldn't let lack of funds deter him or his goals. But if his setbacks don't have to be about money, he'll be able to focus all that genius energy into making the world better.

It's probably silly to struggle the last eleven years like I have, but I promised myself when Sawyer was born that I wouldn't let Nathan shoulder the financial responsibility of raising a kid, even though he'd already signed a generous contract right out of high school. I promised I'd do whatever I had to in order to provide for Sawyer. It's been tight and we haven't had many extras, but we've made it.

"The contract is only for one season. That's fifteen episodes. We'd each be making over seventeen thousand an episode. Between the four of us, that's a million dollars in one season. Granted, taxes will have to be taken out, but still." Rory taps the papers. "Drew said he worked with the network to make sure we had an out after one season if we wanted, so even if we just did the one and stopped, we'd be set for years."

That was news to me. I figured the contract was only one season just in case we sucked. Was Drew really looking out for us like he said?

"Dee, we can't pass this up." Sadie reaches over and stills my hand as I decimate the onion. "I know you don't want to do this, but we can't do it without you. They want all of us or none."

I glance out the window at Sawyer as he plays with Lazurus and his pet fox, Hope. Doing this would not only help the kennel, but it'd make things easier at home too. Help me relax a little, not be so stressed with taking care of things. Fifteen episodes, three, maybe four weeks of being followed by Drew and his camera crew didn't seem so bad in light of all that.

"Okay." I pull my hand from beneath Sadie's and scrape the onion into the bowl with the tomatoes. "I'll do it."

Sadie claps and gives Rory a hug as they squawk in excitement. Snatching the platter of fish, I make a beeline for the grill on the porch. I may have agreed to it, but I still hate the idea.

Chapter Nine

-*DREW*-

I'm pulling into Denali's driveway, not sure what I'll say. *Hey, Denali, can Sawyer play?* Or how about, *Is it okay if Sawyer and I hang out?*

Both sound either pathetic or creepy. Maybe both. The truth is that I was sitting in my rental cottage, completely bored and lonely. I could've gone with Bo and Craig, my cameramen, to dinner, but … I don't know … I just didn't want to go anywhere public.

I know, right? Looks like I am pathetic. I'm lonely but don't want to be with people.

Not true completely, because all I could think about while I pitifully stared out the window was how much I wanted to come visit with Sawyer and see how the falcon healed.

Yeah, okay, maybe I wouldn't mind catching a glimpse of Denali in her relaxed state too. When I close my eyes, I don't see her all put together like she is at the kennel with her hair up in a clip and dressed in jeans and a North STAR polo. None of the other Wilde's wear it, but every time I've seen her there, she'd been in it. So, why does she pop up in my head in leggings, a Sesame Street T-shirt, and messy bun?

Denali's SUV isn't in the driveway, and my heart sinks. If they aren't home, what will I do? I don't want to go back to the little one-room cottage I'm staying in until I find a place to buy. Yet, hanging out on the porch seems a little disturbing.

I let out a breath when I notice Sawyer's bike, then chide myself. I'm putting way too much into this if seeing a kid's bike makes me light, like I've shucked my shell or something. Going home and pulling up Netflix is probably the smarter course, but my feet trek their way to the house anyway.

Muttering from the back yard veers me to the gate. I peer through the lattice and find Sawyer sitting cross-legged, leaning up against his crates, crying. Lazarus and Hope both have their heads in Sawyer's lap. Oh, no. Did the falcon not make it?

"Sawyer?" I open the gate and rush into the back yard. "What's wrong?"

His ears turn red as he wipes his face across his sleeves. "Nothing. I'm fine."

"You're not fine, mate." I ease to the grass next to him. "Did the falcon take a turn for the worse?"

He shakes his head and drops his chin to his chest. So, not the bird. Was he bullied? Get hurt? I scan what I can see of him, and he doesn't seem injured. His fingers slowly brush through his companions' fur, and he's sniffing like his nose has sprung a leak.

I don't know much about kids. Spending the last seven years traveling hasn't given me time around them aside from occasionally at events or in villages where we were shooting. Not knowing what to say, I keep my trap shut. Either he'll start talking or something brilliant will come to me…hopefully.

After what seems like forever, Sawyer finally talks. "My dad just called."

"Oh?" I try to keep chill, but all my hackles rise at those four words. How many phone calls with my dad growing up ended with me crying in my closet? Too many to count.

"Yeah. He got traded, which is awesome. It's everything we've wanted. It's just …" His voice trails off, and my teeth clench so tight my cheeks hurt. He takes a shuddering breath and continues. "They're making him work through the summer, so he won't be coming home."

At the last word, Sawyer crumples into tears. His small shoulders bend over and sobs heave them. I want to find Nathan Blaine and beat the crap out of him. I doubt I'd be able to do much damage, with him being a hockey star and all, but my anger would get me at least one solid punch in.

I slide my hand along Sawyer's shoulders and squeeze. No words at this moment can make this better. Experience has taught me that. But I'm not about to let him go through this alone like I had to. He may be a genius, but he's still just a kid.

When he curls into my side and grabs my shirt in his small hand, my eyes sting. I don't even try to stop the tear that slides down my cheek. I need to fix this, to somehow make up for his dad being a deadbeat. Sawyer's summer won't be ruined, not if I can help it.

After a good five minutes or so, Sawyer's crying stops, and he sits up with a sigh. "I know it doesn't seem like it, but I'm really proud of my dad and this new position." He glances up at me and shrugs, his reddened eyes really popping against his auburn hair and freckles. "We've been dreaming about this for years."

My disgust at Nathan deepens even more. What kind of selfish person convinces their son that living their dream is better than being with family? I don't care that I've only thrown two punches in my life, I'd kick the snot out of him if I could.

"I'm used to seeing him only once a month or so during the season, but summer is usually our time to be together a lot." Sawyer lifts the three-legged, one-eyed fox into his arms and scratches behind her ear. "He promises to come up every day he has off. He just doesn't know when that will be."

"Well, I hope he can figure something out." I try to keep the bitterness from my voice. Sawyer's peek at me says I failed, so I smile. "How's the falcon doing?"

Sawyer's face lights up, and I'm glad I changed the subject. "Frightful is doing awesome."

I can't help the chuckle. "Frightful, huh?"

He tilts his head, his cheeks pinking.

"*My Side of the Mountain* is one of my favorite books, too." I don't want him embarrassed around me. "I named my pet hedgehog Frightful. Not nearly as cool as having an actual falcon, though."

"I don't know. Hedgehogs are pretty amazing." He puts Hope down and stands. "Did you know that they aren't indigenous to the US or Australia for that matter? They also are immune to snake bites. Isn't that crazy? They could actually beat a snake in a fight and eat it."

"Not my Frightful." I give Lazarus a scratch as I stand. "Frightful was the right name to pick for her, just the wrong spelling. She was scared of everything. Once I put live crickets in her cage, and she fainted."

"What?" Sawyer's high-pitched laugh eases my ruffled feathers.

"Yep. I think she was part opossum or something."

"That's funny." He shakes his head then motions toward the house. "Want to come see my Frightful?"

"I reckon."

I follow him into the house. It's picked up a little since the other day. Frightful's box sits on the table still, though Denali's paperwork is gone. I peer in, and the chick gives us a happy chirp.

"She's a beaut." I trace the back of my finger down her head and along her sides which have filled out. "She's right chunky. You're doing a great job with her."

She lifts up her mouth and squawks obnoxiously. Sawyer rolls his eyes and moves to the kitchen. He opens the fridge as he talks.

"The only bad thing about baby birds is how noisy they are." He comes back with a pint jar of brown goo, snagging a medicine dropper from the drawer on his way. "They aren't happy to see you for you. They're happy to see you because you feed them."

He fills the dropper with whatever concoction he has and drops it into the waiting mouth. His motions are slow and deliberate. This kid is an amazing vet.

"She takes it cold?" I squat down so I can watch her more closely.

"I talked to one of the vets at the Anchorage Zoo last time we were up there, and they said it doesn't matter if it's warm or cold as long as the food has the nutrients the chick needs. With how much she eats, it's too much work to warm it up." He sets the food aside and lifts her carefully from the box. "Can you check her side? I think it's healing, but I'd like your opinion on it."

"Sure thing." I lift the wing and peek at her side. It's scabbing around the edges nicely. "Looks great. She'll be in tiptop shape in no time."

"Good." He smiles in relief and places her back in the box. "Want an ice cream bar or something? They're the cheap ones, so they aren't great. Mom saves buying the good ones for special occasions."

Why would Denali need to buy cheap ice cream? Did Nathan not pay child support, or had all extra money gone into starting the kennel?

"I never turn down ice cream, mate." I clap Sawyer on the back.

We wash our hands, grab an ice cream from the freezer, and head to the front porch. While we're walking through the house, I send a quick text to Denali to let her know I'm here.

Hey. I stopped by to see if the falcon was doing okay, and Sawyer was upset about his dad. Is it okay if I hang out on the front porch with him for a while?

Is he okay?

He is now.

Yeah. Okay. That's fine. I'll be home as soon as I can be.

Sawyer plops on the swing, and I ease in next to him. The silence here is different than at the cottage. Fuller somehow. I know it's not the swing but the company, yet when I find a place of my own, I'm putting in a porch swing.

"Thanks for being here." Sawyer's soft words pierce the quiet and punch me in the gut.

This kid's whole world just got toppled, and yet he's glad I'm here?

"Thanks for letting me," I whisper past the lump in my throat.

I never meant to become like Vic, but here I am with an eleven-year-old boy quickly becoming my best friend. Unlike Vic, I'm not going to let my attraction for Denali go any further. Sawyer's had enough disappointments, and I'm not about to add another.

Chapter Ten

-Denali-

It's been three days since Drew sent the text telling me my son had been in tears. Three days since I came home to the two of them sitting on the front porch, talking like old friends. Drew's become an almost constant in Sawyer's life, coming over whenever he's not planning the upcoming shoots for the show.

Well, I guess I don't actually know if Drew's spending all his down time with Sawyer. It's not like I have a tracker on Drew or anything. He could be hanging out with his cameramen Bo and Craig just as much, for all I know. It only seems like he's here all the time.

Oddly, I'm not freaked out by that.

Which means my Mom-radar needs a tune up.

I should be wanting Sawyer to play with kids his own age, not thrilled he's hanging out with a thirty-some-thing-year-old. Only, Sawyer's never had many friends his age. In fact, since about fourth grade, he's only had one friend, Cara. It's fine. Better to have one friend who's solid than a bunch who couldn't care less. The only problem is she spends every summer with her family gold mining. In the past, it hasn't been a big deal since Nathan spent the summer here.

Is it wrong that I'm glad Drew's here to take Sawyer's loneliness away?

As much as Sawyer loves coming to the kennel, there's not much there that he enjoys doing. Unless one of the dogs is sick. Then, he'll spend hours there. Sick dogs are a rare occurrence, praise the Lord, so him hanging out at the kennel all summer, helping us train was never going to happen. Drew staying in Seward to shoot the show will get Sawyer through at least half of the summer. Hopefully by the time Drew leaves, Nathan will figure out a way to be home more.

From my spot on the couch, I glance into the kitchen at Sawyer and Drew chatting with someone on the computer. A friend of Drew's needed his advice on an animal, and, instead of just taking the call at his place, he drove over here so Sawyer could join in. Who does that?

No one, that's who.

Drew doesn't have the superstar ego I pegged him for. In fact, I had him all wrong.

Sawyer leans back in his chair, his hand rubbing his chin in thought. He looks so grown up I want to cry or start taking pictures nonstop so I can keep him little forever. Drew glances at Sawyer and holds up his finger to his friend talking on the computer.

"Sawyer, looks like you've got an idea, mate," Drew asks just like he would another colleague, and my opinion of him rises even more.

"Well, I'm wondering if it's something in her food?"

Sawyer's voice is hesitant and his eyes dart to Drew and back to the computer, like he's worried he's going to let Drew down.

"That's a great thought, but we've changed up her food, trying every different rodent we can get." The person on the computer has that placating tone that people give to kids.

Drew holds his hand up again as he studies Sawyer's face. "Go on."

"Well, it's just that maybe it's not the rodent but what you're feeding the rodent." Sawyer keeps his eyes on Drew, his voice increasing in strength and confidence when Drew nods. "I had a hawk I was helping once who got sick every time I fed him. Threw up all over his cage, which was just nasty."

Sawyer shudders, making Drew laugh. The rich, deep sound slides down my spine and settles warm and tempting in my gut. The two of them look so happy and at ease with each other. I'm quickly discovering that Drew's the type of guy that will be an amazing dad. He doesn't coddle or treat Sawyer like an inferior. But he also brings a levity with him that makes you want to stick around.

Not that I'm thinking of him sticking around or anything.

Okay, maybe the thought has crossed my mind a time or two since he started to come over. It's not a thought I'm willing to entertain. Most importantly, I couldn't get Sawyer's hopes up that his mom would end up with his hero. Less importantly, but only slightly, can you imagine the flack I'd get for my name going from Wilde to Wilder? It'd never stop.

So, I swallow any notion of Drew, aside from friendship, down into the Pit of Not Happening faster than a humpback downing a school of krill. Letting myself imagine anything more with him past the shooting of the show is foolish, and I'm no longer a fool.

"I tried everything." Sawyer's excitement builds as he talks about the hawk, and his hands wave animatedly in the air. "I even had Mom post on Facebook for people to live trap their voles for me to come and get. I biked around town so much, picking up those little buggers, my legs hurt for days."

Drew glances over at me. His eyes twinkle and a dimple on one cheek is visible underneath his five o'clock shadow. My heart flips, arching painfully up my throat like a salmon breaking the water's surface.

Don't be a fool. Don't be a fool.

Heart firmly back in place, I shake my head and roll my eyes. Drew's smile widens, then turns back to Sawyer. I let out a breath I didn't realize I held. Crisis averted. Not letting my emotions get the better of me is harder than I ever imagined. Good thing Drew's only here for a month, six weeks tops. Keeping that in the forefront will make it easier to keep things friendly.

"Anyways, nothing helped." Sawyer pauses, letting the drama build. "Nothing helped that is until I changed the diet of the rodents. Once I did that, I could feed the hawk any animal I could get. Something in the mouse food wasn't agreeing with the hawk."

He makes a face like it's no big deal and slumps back into his chair.

"Crikey, that's a brilliant idea." Drew claps Sawyer on the shoulder and turns to the computer. "Have you tried that, mate?"

"No, no we haven't, but we're going to. Thanks,

Sawyer." Awe replaces the placating tone of earlier. "Kid, if you ever want an internship, you have Drew give me a call. We'd love to have you join us here in Peru any time."

"Wow. Thanks." Sawyer's smile is so big tears blur my vision.

I blink to clear them before anyone notices. Drew is giving Sawyer so much more than friendship. He's building up Sawyer's confidence and giving him experiences he never would have otherwise.

Drew's also making it very easy to let my guard down and relax. It's a good thing he's not divvying up any of that charm on me. After that first night he came over, all attempts to take things further with me came to a screeching halt. I totally get it. Dating a single mom is dangerous ground, even for someone who made their career on diving into the perilous. I'm just glad he didn't stop his friendship with Sawyer too.

Drew shuts the computer and rubs his hands together. "Whelp, I think a celebratory dessert is in order."

"You always think it's a good time for ice cream." Sawyer rolls his eyes as he moves to the fridge.

"That's because it is. Ice cream is perfect for any occasion whether happy or sad. Back me up on this, Dee?" Drew uses my family's nickname like it's an everyday occurrence, and I almost drop my tablet as I'm standing to help.

I blink at him, hoping coherent thought returns quickly. I'm more than a little worried over how a tiny nickname can stall my brain so completely.

"Huh?" It's no use. My brain has short-circuited.

"Ice cream. It can be beneficial in any circumstance,

right?" His eyebrows push together slightly as he studies me.

I just shrug and set the tablet on the kitchen table, hoping to cover my distraction with nonchalance. I know Alaskans are supposed to love their ice cream. We eat more of the cold dessert per capita than any other state. For me, it gets an occasional indulgence that more and more I don't really enjoy. Probably because the stuff I buy is more artificial flavoring than real food. The last few nights, I've savored the treat, but, then again, Drew had brought over the good stuff. You know, the kind you only buy for special events, and only then if it's on sale?

"Mom doesn't really like ice cream." Sawyer says it like I'm the weirdest person alive.

"I like it okay. It's just not my favorite dessert." I grab the scooper and spoons from the drawer.

"What is your favorite, then?" Drew's question turns my attention to him.

Is this a digging question or just a surface conversation question? Does it matter? Nope. Not one bit.

Reaching for the bowls in the cupboard, I pause on my answer. "You know, I'm not sure." I shift my bottom jaw to the side as I set the bowls down on the counter. "I like dessert. I just can't think of something I could eat every night like you seem to with ice cream."

"It's because you haven't found the right flavor yet." Drew plops a huge scoop of deep, rich brown in the top bowl. "When you react the way you do when you drink your cinnamon latte, then we'll know we've discovered your favorite ice cream."

He hands me the bowl, then fills the second. Why has he noticed the way I drink my coffee? I frown at the mound of cold chocolate cradled in my hands. What kind of weird expression do I have that makes it obvious I not only love my latte but am addicted? Great. Now I'm going to stress every time I take a drink.

I jab my spoon into the ice cream and take a bite. Good. The chocolate has the taste of fudge with a hint of hazelnut. It's definitely better than anything I've ever bought, but I couldn't eat it every day.

"Hmm." Drew hands Sawyer his bowl.

"What?" I turn to him and lean against the counter.

"Nothing." He adds a third scoop to his bowl, the massive ball teetering precariously to one side.

"It's not your flavor," Sawyer answers with a shrug.

"How do you know that?" My head ping pongs back and forth between them.

Drew winks at Sawyer, then plops the lid on the carton with his mouth kicking up a fraction on one side. As he puts the carton in the freezer, he asks Sawyer about the process he used to test his theory about the rodent food and the hawk, completely ignoring my question. Drew pulls me into the conversation as the topic slides from one thing to the next. Yet, two hours later as he waves goodbye on his way to the door, the question of how he knew with only a glance that wasn't my flavor still circles.

Chapter Eleven

-*DREW*-

Knocking on the door, I shift from one foot to the other. The tub of ice cream is cold in my hands, making me wish I'd put it in a bag. I really shouldn't get such a kick out of Denali trying new flavors, but it's become an obsession—that doesn't sound right. More like a mission. A not-so-secret mission.

I shouldn't pay attention to her like I do, especially since I'm keeping things firmly in the friend zone. It's my consolation prize for putting a stop on pursuing the woman of my dreams. There, I said it. She's incredible, more amazing than I first realized. She's smart, often reading for hours on end about training and business stuff. She's got motherhood down to an art, with just the right balance of freedom and caring that gives Sawyer what he needs to soar.

Sawyer opens the door, and a big smile fills his face. You know what? I don't need a consolation prize. Not with the friendship I've gained from this kid.

"G'day, mate." Sawyer's attempt at Strine is spot on.

I answer in my best American, which comes out like an odd mix between Boston and Texan accents. "Howdy, partner."

No one ever claimed I was a great actor.

Sawyer collapses against the doorframe in laughter. "That was horrible."

"Oi! That was a right bonzer attempt." I nudge his shoulder as I walk by, making him laugh even harder.

"What's so funny?" Denali asks as she comes down the stairs.

"Drew's attempt at sounding American." Sawyer snorts, making me smile though I'm trying to keep a look of indignation on my face. "You should do it for my mom."

I'm already shaking my head. "You must think I'm nutty as a fruit cake."

"No, just horrible at accents." Sawyer wipes his fingers under his eyes.

If I can make him laugh with bad impersonations, then I'm game. The truth is, because of my father, I never wanted anything to do with acting. Never tried out for plays. Never pretended to be a cowboy or a soldier or anything else. My father does enough pretending for the both of us, and I never wanted anything that resembled him in my life growing up.

The irony of me making my living from being in front of the camera isn't lost on me. I made sure every shot, every interaction with guests was real. We faked nothing on my show. Sometimes I wonder if it was enough or if giving in to the lure of the camera made me more like my father than I like? He definitely enjoyed the added exposure my fame brought to him, even if it was second hand and I still refuse to have anything to do with him.

"No." Sadie's firm voice yanks me from my thoughts.

She's standing at the counter scowling at me. Her hand holds a knife poised over vegetables on the cutting board. I glance at Violet at the stove behind her for help. She just shrugs and smiles.

"What?" I have no clue what I've done wrong.

"No more ice cream." Sadie points the knife at the carton like it's a deadly animal she needs to fend off.

"Um. You want me to take it back?" I take a step toward the door.

"There's no room in the freezer for real food, let alone more ice cream." Sadie sets the knife down and crosses her arms over her chest.

"I'll go put it in the deep freezer." Denali grabs it, her fingers skimming mine.

My heart skips a beat at the touch. It's so brief, there shouldn't be any reaction from me, but there is. Which means I need to be even more diligent in keeping a safe distance. You pile enough of those reactions on me, and I'll lose my focus. Veer down a one-way track to Denali-ville.

"There's no room in that freezer either." Sadie throws up her hands. "What's the deal with our house suddenly becoming an ice cream parlor anyways?"

"We're trying to figure out Mom's favorite flavor." At least Sawyer taking part of the blame keeps me from looking like a creeper, because the itchiness under my skin at the question makes me uncomfortable.

"Really?" Violet's eyes light up, and she wags her eyebrows at me.

"It's nothing." I frown at her and shake my head. Can't have them thinking there's more to it than there is.

Now, though, I'm thinking I've put too much in this entire flavor thing. I really shouldn't go to the shop each evening and stare at the shelves of flavors, wondering what Denali will like. It shouldn't take me ten minutes to decide each time. I need to tone it down, wait until one kind is gone before I get another.

"We should have a game night." Sawyer plops on the stool at the counter and snags a carrot slice from the cutting board. "Invite everyone over for ice cream and charades."

"That sounds like a blast." Violet snatches her phone from the counter, sliding her finger across the screen. "I'm texting Kemp. He was just talking about how he's been so busy with the boat he hasn't seen anyone in forever."

From what I can tell, Violet's friend Kemp is also somewhat new to the area. Not only does he own a fishing charter, but he's also a world-famous snowboarder and does search and rescue with Violet and Sadie. I hope he'll come over, because I've been wanting to talk to him about taking Sawyer out on the boat to look for animals someday soon.

"What are we doing?" Denali comes in from the garage as Sadie grabs her phone.

"Game night!" Sawyer holds both fists in the air in victory.

"We have some finger food in the deep freezer. We can make that too." Denali turns to me. "Think your cameramen would want to come over? They're probably getting bored with Seward by now."

"Really?" See what I mean?

Not only does she take the lonely Aussie in, but she invites his friends as well. She's a ripper, all right. I'm in so much trouble.

"Of course." Denali's face scrunches like I'm a loon for asking.

A phone rings, and Sawyer scrambles to answer it. Nathan's face pops up on the video chat. My hands ball into fists. I still can't get the image of Sawyer crying over Nathan ditching him out of my head. Stepping into the living room to call Bo and Craig, I hope the move hides the fact that I'm no longer a Nathan Blaine fan.

I give the guys the invite and directions. The entire time, though, my attention glues to Sawyer chatting animatedly with Nathan. Denali comes back into the kitchen and goes straight to Sawyer's side to get in on the conversation. They don't look like a family divided, not with the way all their laughter fills the house. Even Violet and Sadie get in on the conversation, giving Nathan a hard time about being a wimp because he's having trouble adjusting to the altitude of Denver.

Ending the call with the guys, I just stare into the kitchen. My mind can't seem to wrap around the reality laid out before me. No matter what Sawyer and Denali insisted, I've imagined Nathan just like my dad.

Selfish.

Deadbeat.

Not worth wasting a nanosecond of thought over.

But what's going on before me doesn't mesh with that image. If Denali and Nathan get along so well, why didn't they stay together? Denali moves to the kitchen to help Violet and Sadie. Sawyer focuses on Nathan. The loneliness in Nathan's voice is unmistakable. What's keeping him from coming back and reclaiming his family? That beaut of a thought twists in my gut and leaves me chilled.

Chapter Twelve

-Denali-

Pressing my arms to my side, I groan as I cross the parking area to the network van. Of course, today, the day of my first solo episode for the network, had to be the hottest day of the summer so far. My shirt armpits are soaked, like huge wet, rings soaked. I really should've brought another top or ordered extra-strength antiperspirant from Amazon or something. Violet's hippie, homemade stuff isn't cutting it today. At least I went with the white polo. The sweat circles hopefully won't show up so bad.

"Hey, Denali." Drew crosses to me, waddling in the dog bite training suit.

My mouth does this rolling motion as I get my smirk under control. He looks ridiculous and, yet, still handsome as all get-out. At least we'll both end the day in a sweaty mess. Though, my luck, he'll probably pop out of the suit later all crisp and sweat-free.

"I saw that." He wags his finger at me, and my smile breaks free.

Defiant smile.

Doesn't it know I'm still trying to keep my guard up around this man? It's hard, harder than I thought it would be. He's been so good for Sawyer the last week. In fact, Drew barely talks to me at all. He's not rude or anything, just more focused on hanging out with my kid than me.

At first, I worried that Drew was using Sawyer to soften me up. But the more Drew came around, the more he interacted with Sawyer, the more I realized Drew genuinely likes being with my son. It's good for him, especially after Nathan dropped the news. Now, though, I'm worried that I might be the one using Drew. I mean, he comes over on his own, but I'm definitely encouraging the friendship, hoping having Drew around for the next few weeks will take the sting away a little from Nathan being gone.

Then my worry turns to what will happen with Sawyer when Drew leaves. I swallow and push the thought aside. I can't think about that right now, maybe not until the time comes for us to cross that bridge.

"Sorry." I straighten my mouth back into submission.

"No wuckas. I reckon I look like an overstuffed koala."

His laugh bounces so easily from him, I wonder if it ever dries up. I noticed that this week when he was with Sawyer and the first episode we shot with Sadie in the park. He's quick to make others feel comfortable, primarily by his easy smile and willingness to laugh at himself.

"You look hot." When my comment has his eyebrows wagging up and down and his smile turning cheeky, I quickly add, "Like temperature hot, not hot, good-looking hot."

What am I even saying?

"Not that you aren't good-looking or anything. You just have to be roasting in there." My pulse pounds a command in my ears with each frantic beat. *Stop. Talking. Stop. Talking.*

"Nah, it's not too bad." He pauses as he leans closer and drops his voice to a whisper. "Especially since I'm practically in the nuddy."

"What?" Why do so many Aussie terms sound like baby talk?

"Well, I'm wearing a budgie smuggler."

"Aah. That really cleared it up." I roll my eyes, glad for the distraction from my embarrassment and nerves.

"What? You've never heard of a Speedo?" He truly looks shocked.

His words register, and I find myself glancing up and down his body like I have X-ray vision or something. I'm not usually a fan of the obnoxious swimwear, but I bet my favorite cinnamon latte that Drew looks amazing in one. When I reach his face, he wags his eyebrows again and winks. My chest flushes, and instantly my ears are hotter than shrimp on a barbie. Do Australians even say that?

"Great." I cross my arms and pierce him with a glare, like I'm not dying of embarrassment. "We'll have to get a new suit now."

He tips his head back and laughs. It bounces down my shoulders and back, relaxing me with each skip. With a quick motion, he pulls me toward him.

"Come here, ya." It's like hugging Baymax from Sawyer's favorite move, *Big Hero 6*, and while it should smell sharp and pungent, Drew's spicy scent covers me in tummy-swirling warmth.

"Ew. Get off." I push him away. I don't want or need any movement in my core that signals attraction, especially since I seem to have fallen off his radar.

"All right, Dee, ready to sic the dog after me?" His use of my nickname sends my tummy into another back flip, and I mentally chide the stupid organ.

"Oh, yeah." I put a little too much excitement into my response. Can't help it. I love this part of the training.

His eyes look nervous as they dart to me. Good. I won't be the only one anxious.

"Remember, I'm using a beginner dog today, which is why you're in the full suit. I've only had him a couple of weeks, so go easy on him." I walk backward toward my SUV.

"Me go easy on him?" Drew twists left and right in the suit. "He needs to go easy on me."

I get Hercules, the German Shepard, from the crate, and we shoot the intro into the episode. Once Drew starts asking me questions as I talk him through what we're doing, all my nerves vanish like mist on the mountains in the morning sun. I might even have a film of salt left on my skin, which isn't as appealing when it's sweat as when it's ocean water.

We get to the part where I'm going to send Herc to bite and hold Drew's arm. A bead of sweat trails down his face. His expression has turned serious, like he's actually nervous.

Drew looks straight into the camera. "Okay, mates. You ready? I'm about to catch a bite."

Waddling to the center of the field we are working

in, he turns and takes a breath. I want to tell him it's not going to hurt, but becoming a dog's chew toy isn't pleasant. He bounces on his toes and tries to clap his hands. They stop about six inches from connecting, so he throws a thumbs up instead.

I tunnel vision my focus, forgetting the cameras, my anxiety, how impossible it is that Drew looks sexy as an inflated sumo wrestler. Hercules is my only concern, so I need to push all that other stuff down. I can't let my feelings confuse him. He needs my calm reassurance to get this job done.

"Okay, Herc, fass." I motion him toward Drew.

The dog bolts across the field, and I race after him. Drew's eyes widen, then squeeze shut a moment before Herc connects. At the last second, the dang dog veers his course and grabs Drew right in the crotch. Drew's eyelids snap open, his face a contortion of shock and pain, as he falls backward with a squeal. As soon as Drew crashes to the ground, Hercules is living up to his name and dragging Drew across the dirt.

"Herc, aus." My command to let go is sharp, and, thankfully, the dog responds. "Oh, good boy. You got that bad man."

I rub the dog down, talking all kinds of encouragement to him even though Drew is lying lifeless on the ground next to me. The dog's training could be messed up if I don't reward him. I take out a ball from my cargo pocket and toss it across the field. When Herc takes off after it, I kneel next to Drew.

His face is scrunched tight. Bo, the cameraman, circles around so he can see us both. I guess getting the shot is important, like making sure the dog is trained properly. Poor Drew.

"How's the budgie smuggler now?" I have no clue what possesses me to say that. It's like my worry that he's seriously hurt and the humor in the situation tumbles the words out of my mouth.

"Peachy. Never been better." He groans and tries to roll over.

It's like watching a turtle flipped on its shell. Drew's arms flail but all he does is wiggle back and forth. A snort escapes me, and I slap my hand over my mouth to stop the laughter, but it pushes out in a sound that is way too close to a fart. Drew stops his struggling, the entire suit shaking with his chuckling. Hercules drops the ball next to Drew's head and licks the poor, defenseless man on the face.

"Good on ya, mate." Drew leans his head into the doggie kisses, his voice full of joy.

The guard around my heart gets even more flimsy. It started out good and sturdy, like an eight-foot privacy fence. Each time Drew visits with my son, a little more height gets sheared off the top. Drew's lack of anger at the dog and obvious love of animals turns that guard into a chain-link fence. You know the kind with those dinky, plastic pieces threaded through the open spaces? Not very protective. And, despite my brain screaming for me to reinforce my defenses, I'm not sure I want to build the fence back up.

Chapter Thirteen

-*DREW*-

I'm not sure it's safe for me to be driving right now. My brain bounces so many ways—from the fact that I just bought property in Alaska to Denali's quick acceptance to come see a surprise to how easy it is to be with Denali and Sawyer—that I can barely keep my mind on the road. Between tourists and people flocking to fish for salmon, Seward during the summer is not a good time to daydream while driving.

Denali and Sawyer chat back and forth about the two otter pups that the Sea Life Center rescued yesterday. He'd told us all about them last night while we ate popsicles in the Wilde's back yard. He'd been hoping to get a peek at them today, and from his excitement, I guess the little bugger found a way behind the scenes.

"Ah, look how cute they are." Denali twists in the passenger seat next to me so she can see Sawyer in the back.

She grabs Sawyer's phone and turns it to me. Sure

enough, Sawyer's picture is up close and personal with the pups. Definitely not a twenty-five buck tour shot.

"How'd ya get in the back?" I flip on the blinker to head down Nash Street.

"I talked with Susie. She's the education director."

"Sawyer." Denali's tone turns parental.

Is that a tone you automatically get when you become a parent, or does it take practice?

"What? She was totally okay with showing me." Sawyer's face in the rearview mirror is the classic innocent look.

"You know you aren't supposed to use our friendship to get you in like that." She hands the phone back to him, then turns to me. "Susie has been one of my best friends since high school. She has a soft spot for Sawyer, and he knows it."

I don't blame the woman. Sawyer is an easy kid to love. I doubt Sawyer actually uses that to his advantage, not in a wheedling way, at least. He just gets excited about animals.

"I know, Mom, but there hasn't been an otter pup in so long, and now there's two."

"Okay, okay. Just don't make a habit of it, and wait until Susie calls you to go visit again." Denali slumps in the seat and looks around. "Where are you taking us?"

"Well…"

I'm still not sure how she's going to react to me permanently setting up shop here. I've really put my best effort at pushing my attraction to her into the depths of my emotional reef, so to speak. I think I've done a banging job of it, but the effort has me stuffed. Tired out. It wouldn't be so exhausting if she wasn't such a battler. I'm rooting for her at every new turn.

I pass the Seward City Church and turn on the next drive. The trees growing tall along the dirt road darken the interior, but I can still feel her gaze on me. Questioning. There's no hiding anymore.

"Well, I'd like to show you my new place." I peek at her and smile, hoping the expression takes away some of the shock.

"Your new place?" Her words come out slow and drawn out, like sap oozing down a spruce.

We pull out of the trees into the open area. I know the run-down buildings and open gravel lot don't look like much, but, to me, it's all my dreams finally within grasp. Well, not all. I force myself not to look at Denali. I stop at the main building and turn off the car.

"You bought a house?" Denali's staring out the window, darting her eyes about.

"Kind of. Well, not really." I twist in my seat so I can look at both of them. "I bought this place to open up a rescue center for animals here."

"Cool!" Sawyer opens the door and hurries out. "I want to see."

I have one person on my side, not that I doubted he'd be stoked.

"I don't understand." Denali shakes her head.

"My dream has always been to help animals, to have a place where I could fix them enough to release them back into the wild. That was my goal in vet school." I sigh and scan the property. "It was the reason I took the job with Nature, so I could actually fund my dream."

"So, you'll open up a center and hire people while you do your regular life?" She shrugs. "That's a pretty good idea. I mean, you can tell with Sawyer's little clinic in the back yard that there are lots of animals that need help." She turns to me. Her tone is accepting but her expression is shuttered, blank. "Would you focus on a specific animal?"

"No."

"That will keep things interesting."

"No, I mean I'll be running things. I'm sticking around."

Here it goes. Reality is about to crash down on me. I'll finally know what Denali really thinks.

She blinks and her voice falters. "What?"

My stomach drops, and I turn from her. Disappointment feels a lot like a boat ride on choppy waters. Heart rising in excitement, only to crash down with nauseating force.

"After your show ends, I'm done with Nature. My contract for my show came up for renewal this past winter, but I didn't sign. For years, I've been searching for where I wanted to open. When I drove into Seward that first time, I just knew I wouldn't be leaving." I force a chuckle. "My mum is a little cranky about me not going back to Oz."

"So, you're not leaving?" She's fiddling with her necklace, watching Sawyer turn in a slow circle.

"Nope." I push open the door, needing to move to dispel the disenchantment threatening to settle on me. "You've got yourself a new neighbor."

I get out and purposely close the door with a soft click. Knowing you shouldn't get your hopes up and doing it must be a monumental task. Here I am, my property crunching beneath my feet, my dream forming perfectly in my head with each building, and I'm upset because the woman I thought was a friend isn't happy I'm staying.

Oh, how the mighty fall.

"Drew, you're opening a center here?" Sawyer motions with his hands to the creek pouring into Resurrection Bay and the open view beyond the property line that stretches across Resurrection River to the main part of Seward.

"Yeah. That's the plan." I shove my hands into my pockets, trying to relax and let his excitement replace the disappointment.

"Just like we talked about?" He turns to me, hope beaming from his face.

I had told him of my dream, told him that I've wanted to help animals, like he's doing, since I was a kid. I just never had the nerve to set one up in my back yard. It's funny how we both have the same dream. Watching Sawyer, I wish I would've been brave enough to start earlier.

"Yeah, mate. This place needs a lot of work before I can bring in animals, though."

He jumps up and down. "This is totally wicked."

"Yeah, yeah it is."

My smile returns without me forcing it this time. Okay, so maybe it's not that bad that Denali isn't excited. Sawyer has enough enthusiasm to fuel me and the entire project.

"Here." I toss him the keys to the house. "Let's go see what we've got."

He catches them with a whoop and takes off toward the house. I scan the property again, letting the vision of what I want to do here seep back into me. The soft crunch of steps on gravel can't even evaporate the good vibes tingling through me right now.

"Drew?" Her soft touch on my arm jolts an aware-ness through me that I don't want right now.

I've done pretty good at keeping my distance. I've kept the friends-thing up, making sure I'm focused more on Sawyer than her. I can't hurt him and our friendship by pursuing anything with Denali, so why tempt myself with little touches here and there?

Maybe I would've been better acclimating myself to her more. Brushing her hand when she hands me things instead of carefully grabbing so there's never any skin-on-skin contact. Because right now, the way my entire arm is tingling like I just walked through a patch of stinging nettle isn't doing my cause any good.

"You want to see the house?" I step toward the building like a lizard scurrying to shade.

"Yeah, I do, but first I want to apologize." She rubs her lips with the fingertips of one hand.

"No worries. I kind of shocked you with it." I take another step, but she grips my arm again.

"I guess, I just assumed you'd be leaving, and I've been trying to figure out how to prepare Sawyer for that." She drops her hand with a sigh, and I can finally breathe. "With Nathan not being here for the summer, hanging out with you has helped Sawyer, but I've been worried that when you left, it would break his heart even more. You're staying was such a relief I guess, I didn't know what to say that wouldn't sound selfish."

So, she's happy I'm staying? My thoughts just sort of freeze in my brain. I'm one of those stingrays the Kiwi orcas shock into sleep by flipping upside down. I say the first thing that pops into my head.

"You're not selfish." I pull in a breath through my

nose as my brain flips from stunned to racing speed. "You're one of the most selfless people I've ever met."

She makes a self-deprecating sound. "You wouldn't think so if you could hear my thoughts."

A blush eases up her cheeks. She peeks at me, then quickly looks away. Suddenly, I'm wondering if any of her thoughts toward me are selfish for her and not because of Sawyer.

Chapter Fourteen

-*Denali*-

The smell of marinara and cheese tempts me to open the pizza box and snag a piece before I get to Drew's. I really should've eaten something more for breakfast than a banana and granola bar. Clearly, because I'm so starved, I'm tempted to pull to the side of the road and shove a steaming piece in my mouth.

There's also no way the three of us will eat two extra-large pizzas. I look at the boxes stacked in the passenger seat and cringe. That was a bit excessive, but at least there will be leftovers for Drew later. That is, if I don't bury my face in the box and eat the whole dang thing.

Why, oh why, haven't I learned that training the dogs will suck me into the vortex where nothing but the job exists? You'd think after doing this for the last nine years, granted on a much smaller scale, it would have taught me to eat better. It hasn't. What I really need to do is be like a toddler and pack my pocket full of snacks. I'd have to make sure I don't mix up the pockets with my food and the dogs' treats. Though there are some days I'm so hungry, the bacon biscuit bites might just entice me to try a nibble.

I turn on to the drive, talking my stomach down from a complete revolt. A hundred more feet and it can stop complaining, but I need to get out of the vehicle with some small degree of dignity. Having cheese and sauce dripping from my mouth won't cut it.

Cocking my head as I stop next to a car I don't recognize, I wonder who Drew got to work out here on a Saturday. Granted, most Alaskans work hard all summer, no matter the day. We have to take advantage of the midnight sun while we can. I'm just surprised, since he said he was going to do as much as he could himself before he hired help.

Maybe that means he's further along than he thought he'd be?

Or maybe he ran into some big issues?

Would that discourage him? Buildings in Alaska can sometimes be sketchy as all get out. A lot of places were built before building codes were put in place, and, in some areas, codes don't even exist. So, what looks like a sturdy house at first glance, can end up a mess underneath the skirt, if you know what I mean. I hope this place doesn't become a money pit, and Drew throws in the towel.

I let Hank out of the back seat, circle the car, and pull the pizzas from the passenger door. I may or may not have pushed my nose against the box top and dragged in a big hit. Sometimes a girl has to go to extreme measures to keep her tummy happy. Now it knows lunch is a few moments away, and I can hopefully deliver these circles of deliciousness without incident.

Music blares from the open windows of the house along with the banging of hammers. At the moment, it sounds like that classic rock song *Down Under* by Men at Work, but, really, it could be rock at one moment and country the next. As long as the musician is Aussie, Drew doesn't care what type it is. Lazarus and Hope yip from the back yard as they run to greet Hank. The scene is very much like I'm coming home after a long day.

I shake off the feeling and move toward the house. It's probably due to us spending so much time out here the last week since Drew first showed us and my insane hunger that has all these feelings of possession bubbling up. Definitely doesn't have anything to do with the sexy Aussie who hasn't made a move on me since that first night he asked me out to dinner.

Not one smidgeon of a move.

Hardly even touches me.

"Are you trying to tempt me?" Drew's off-key singing belts from the window as I pass, and I'm dangerously close to answering yes. "Because I come from the land of plenty."

His horrible singing makes me laugh. Well, we have one thing in common aside from loving animals. Personality-wise, we are so completely different. He's all charming and charismatic. I'm duty and loyalty to a fault. He goes out on limbs to get his dreams. I make detailed plans so I don't drop the ball and let my family down. Yet, with the episodes we've been shooting and the work we've done out here, I'm thinking maybe those differences might actually be a good thing.

"Eh, there's a beaut of a sight, if I ever saw one."

An Australian voice I don't recognize shouts from the house. "Mates, there's a beautiful mermaid here to lure us to the depths with grub."

I roll my eyes and glance at my tourist T-shirt for Exit Glacier I got at the secondhand store and ratty, jean shorts. Definitely not mermaid material. With strands of hair blowing in my face from my messy bun, I'm not even pizza delivery person level. In fact, there's a good chance I smell like dog, too, and not the good kind of dog. Hercules rolled in something nasty and needed a bath, so I'm betting I've got that dead animal stink going on.

"Nah, that's just my mom. She's cool and all, but she's just a regular person." Sawyer always makes sure things are based in reality. Gotta give the kid props there.

"Mate, there's nothing normal about your mum. Nothing at all." Drew's quick retort in his deep, rumbling accent makes my legs go all weak, and I almost let the pizza topple into the dirt.

Just what did he mean by that? I know I shouldn't care. I do, okay? Suddenly, I care a lot. More than I want to.

"Mom!" Sawyer barrels out the door, and I shake off the wobbles. "You're here."

He grabs the pizza boxes, kisses me on the cheek—yes, he hasn't gotten to the age where that's no longer okay, and I'm hoping he never gets there—and rushes back into the house. Drew's standing on the porch, shaking his head as Sawyer practically runs past. Drew's hair has bits of sheetrock stuck in it and his shirt is a white, powdery mess, but construction Drew is just as swoon worthy as TV star Drew, maybe more.

"Thanks for bringing lunch." He tips his head toward the inside. "We've survived the morning on soda and trail mix. It'll be nice to have something a little more substantial and not so sugary in our systems."

"That explains Sawyer's overabundance of energy."

"Yeah." Drew cringes. "Sorry about that."

"No wuckas." I wave him off with his own saying, and his eyes sparkle with humor.

We just stand there for a minute staring. Maybe it's just me, but the air definitely gets thick and electric, like the atmosphere shifting before a thunderstorm. Trembles start in my fingers and work their way up my arm.

"Drew, you gonna intro me to your mate?" The voice from earlier snaps through the static like thunder, and I shake my hands to dispel the lingering jitters.

I need to eat before my entire body, not just my stomach, mutinies.

"Vic, this is Sawyer's mum, and my friend, Denali." Well, Drew's introduction puts me right back into place. "Denali, this is my best friend, Vic."

Now, this shocks me. Vic has to be my dad's age, with his graying hair and wrinkles around his eyes and mouth. Don't get me wrong. The man has that whole silver fox thing going, but him being Drew's best friend gives me another little peek into who Drew really is.

What thirty-year-old has a best friend twice their age?

"Ah, mate, now you're making me blush." Vic reaches out his hand to me. There isn't a tinge of pink on his cheeks. "So, you're the woman Sawyer and Drew keep talking about?"

"Depends on what they were saying." I dart my gaze

to Drew as he shakes his head and rubs his fingers over his eyelids like he's getting a headache.

"All good things, I promise." Vic tucks my hand in his elbow and leads me inside. "Why, Drew here was just saying how he's never met anyone like you."

"Vic, I thought you said you popped by unexpectedly to help a mate out, not run your trap." Drew's groan has me wanting to turn to see his expression, but Vic is feeding me some good stuff here, though not as filling as the pizza will be.

"Drew's always been a workhorse. Ever since I first met him when he was six." Vic sighs like it's a bad thing. "The kid always strived to do his best, get the highest grades, help his footy team get the most points."

I'm not sure what footy is. I'm assuming football, since the Aussies seem thrilled with shortening words and throwing a cute ending on it. Now, whether it's football, soccer, or some obscure sport only in Australia, I'll have to ask Drew later.

"You've known Drew since he was six?" I ask the question that is jumping the highest, waving its hand frantically in the air.

"Yep. His mum and I dated for a while." His jovial expression falls before his lips push back up to a smile. "Haven't been able to shake the kid since we broke up."

"Like you wanted to," Drew says with assurance.

"Nope, you're right. I wasn't about to let you go, mate." Vic lets my arm drop and claps Drew on the back. "Now you're stuck with me, including all my embarrassing antics with the ladies. I'm grabbing a cuppa to go with the pizza." Vic winks at me, then heads to the kitchen with a wave. "Nice to finally meet you, Denali."

The way he says finally has those tingles back in my fingers. Drew just shrugs at me with an amused smile and follows Vic into the kitchen. Has Drew been talking about me to Vic before he got here? The question makes me a little lightheaded.

Why would his mom's ex-boyfriend stay friends with a small boy? The little I know about Drew's past I learned from Wikipedia, since he doesn't talk much about himself. At least to me he doesn't. His parents divorced when he was young, and his dad is the famous movie star, Ben Hamilton. Other than the information about his time in college and his TV show, that's all I've got.

I walk into the kitchen to find the three guys laughing about something. I can tell by the way Drew's looking at Vic that he loves him. It's the same way Sawyer looks at Nathan. If I didn't know any better, I'd think Vic was Drew's father, which has me wondering about what caused Vic and Drew's mom to break up all those years ago. Also makes me wonder if there's more to Drew's shift in his attention from me than just not being interested.

My entire body trembles as that thought takes root. Drew tilts his head, his eyebrows drawing together as he watches me. I can tell that he notices something's wrong. Kind of like he's always picking up on things, now that I think of it. Suggesting we go inside in the evening after I shiver. Bringing over new ice cream flavors so he can find my favorite.

I plop into an empty chair, snag a piece of pizza, and shove it into my mouth. I need to really think about this, figure out what it means. Maybe make a list of all the possibilities so I don't jump to any conclusions and do the wrong thing. Because right now, my heart—the one that bleeds loyalty to a fault—is pounding so hard at the implications I might just do something crazy, like find out if that sexy accent of Drew's translates into his kiss.

Chapter Fifteen

-*DREW*-

A cool breeze blows against my hot skin as I yank on another downed limb in the back yard. Sweat pours from my face and soaks my shirt. I'm so rank, I can smell myself. Who knew summers could blister in Alaska?

I peek at Denali from the corner of my eye where she's stacking branches in her arms. I can't tell you how many times I've done that since she arrived earlier with pizza. Not because I'm checking her out or anything.

Okay.

Yeah, mate, you got me.

A few times have definitely been that.

Mostly, though, I'm worried. She looked pale and off-balance in the kitchen earlier. The way she shoved the pizza in her mouth means she probably didn't eat all day. Again. Usually, she just gets cranky. She's never looked like she might pass out before. So, I'm watching her like a hawk.

For a guy who has been trying his darndest to keep his eyes, hands, and thoughts to himself, my brain switched pretty quick to focus mode. I'm just making sure she doesn't collapse from the heat. Yet, I can't help noticing how her hair keeps falling from her bun or how the many shades of auburn pop in the bright light. Her cheeks and nose have pinked from being out in the sun.

She could totally be a mermaid. I want to tell her she can lasso me with seaweed and drag me to her secluded cove any time. I won't, since that would negate what I'm doing with Sawyer.

No lassoing. No checking her out. No noticing how sexy her calves are when she rises on her tiptoes to reach for something.

You know, it would be easier on me if she wore pants … and a parka. Bundle her up in winter gear and I wouldn't have such a hard time. I toss the limb into the burn pile with a grunt. Yeah, that wouldn't work. She'd have to wear a full-face mask, maybe one of those snow-mobile helmets that covers everything.

"Man, it's hot today." She throws her branches into the pile and stretches her shoulders back.

I rip my gaze from her to the pile and wipe my arm across my forehead. "Yep. It's a scorcher."

I peek to see if it's safe to look and find her fanning herself. Sweat drips down her cheek which is blotchy from exertion. She brushes her hand across her skin and grimaces when it comes away wet. Even dirty and sweaty, she's gorgeous. I can't win.

"Break time." I stomp to the gazebo in the center of the small patch of grass behind the house.

She steps up next to me as she pulls off her work

gloves. Seriously, brain. There should be nothing attractive about taking gloves off, but apparently to my gray matter there is.

Just great.

Like my core temp wasn't hot enough. I stop at the table I threw together with plywood and sawhorses, grab a bottle of water from the little cooler, and chug it down. The cold water feels refreshing on my parched throat, but it doesn't help the rest of me much. Denali takes a drink from her bottle and sighs as she puts the cold plastic against her forehead. Any relief my drink gave evaporates with that sound.

I uncap the bottle and pour the entire thing over my head. Denali shrieks as some splashes on her. I love how she's relaxed around me, that I've gone from enemy number one to at least a friend. I shake my head to get her more wet. Her laugh is instant and carefree, at least for the moment, and the fact that I put that there has me flying higher than Denali's summit.

The mountain, not the woman.

I doubt she reaches one-sixty-five centimeters, since she barely skims my chin. Which, by the way, would be the perfect height for hugging.

I toss the empty bottle into the box to be refilled. It's useless. One thought of holding her, and I'm right back to overheated.

"So, Vic." She takes another drink as she looks over her bottle at me. "Did you know he was coming?"

"Nah, at least not right away." I move to the outside of the gazebo that still has a railing. It's more like a board nailed between the beams, but it's sturdy enough for me to lean against. "When I talked to him two days ago, he said he wanted to help. He flew in this morning and drove down from Anchorage. Arrived around ten this morning with a duffle and a cheeky smile."

"He just dropped everything and came? Is he retired?"

"He owns a construction company. It's big enough now that he has other people run it, and he just has to check in."

"That will come in handy, having someone who knows construction helping." She leans against the board next to me.

I look out over the bay at the mountain shooting to the sky behind Seward on the other side of the water. I don't think I'll ever get used to this scene. Maybe if I stare at it long enough, I can remember all the reasons noticing Denali is a bad idea. She shifts next to me and brushes my arm. There goes that thought.

"It's really amazing how close you two are. Did he date your mom long?"

"Eighteen months. They were engaged, and me mum broke it off."

"Why? He seems amazing."

"He is. Broke his heart. Mine too, for that matter."

I avoid talking about my past and childhood as much as possible. So many kids have it worse than I did. I wasn't abused or anything. Just lonely. And confused. Trying to make up for my dad leaving by being the best, working the hardest. I wanted to … needed to keep things easy on my mom, so I hid my disappointments in her decisions, learning to smile through until I could get off on my own.

"What happened?" Denali asks, and I want to tell her.

Friends talk about things, right?

"Well, after my dad left, I guess my mum had a hard time landing again. She's a lot like Violet."

"Spastic and dramatic?" Denali chuckles.

"No, expressive and imaginative. Mum's an artist, creates jewelry out of things in nature, and leans into that persona with flare. I think she lost her spark with my dad. He's egotistical and controlling, and when he left for someone else, mum never quite got over that, especially with how much she changed herself for him." I shake my head as I think about that time. "I was little, but I remember those first few years when he pretended he still cared. Whenever he came around, she'd become this meek version of my mum I didn't recognize. It scared me, made me mad. Just another reason to not like the man."

"I'm sorry. That must've been hard."

"Yeah. Anyway, life looked up when Mum started dating Vic. She'd gone out with a few guys here and there, but none of them stuck like Vic did."

An eagle swoops over the yard, heading out to the water to hunt. I want to do that, just kind of soar away from this conversation. Yet, I can't end it there. It's just not what friends do, and I'm so desperate for true connections right now, I know I can't keep this part of me to myself.

"At the time, I didn't understand why my mum called things off, but looking back I think she was afraid. Vic is the complete opposite of her, business-minded and straight-laced, where she's got the whole Bohemian vibe down. I think she worried she'd meld into his life and lose herself in the process again. So, instead of figuring it out together, she called the whole relationship off."

"But to call off a wedding?" Denali shakes her head. "I couldn't do that to Sawyer. Actually, that's why I don't date. I never want him to get attached to someone and have the relationship not work out."

I want to tell her it was almost worse seeing my mum alone. If she'd let herself trust again, maybe the pressure I had to make her happy wouldn't have been so heavy. Not that she expected me to do it. I just wanted to help her, and making her proud was the only way I knew how.

Denali's talking before I can formulate my response in a way that won't hurt her feelings. "Did either of them ever marry?"

"No. Vic hasn't dated anyone since Mum, and the few guys she went out with didn't last past a second date. Always seem to ask about each other in round about ways, though." Maybe there's something I can do to get them back together.

"How sad. I mean, you're all grown up now, they should just hook up and stop pining over each other." She sucks in a breath and stiffens.

I follow her gaze to a brown bear lumbering down from the road through the grass next to the house. Bears are just a part of life living here where the salmon run, but for it to be coming through the yard where dogs are is not normal. Hank and Lazarus bark in the house, and my heart pounds in my chest.

"The dogs." Denali steps forward, but I put my hand on her arm to stop her when the bear snuffs and turns its head our direction.

I pull my phone from my pocket and call Vic. "Vic, keep the dogs and Sawyer inside."

"What? These dogs are going nuts."

"Keep them inside. There's a bear out here," I whisper into the phone, praying I don't draw the bear's attention.

"Son, are you all right?"

"Yeah. Just keep Sawyer inside okay?"

"On it. Start yelling if it decides it wants a snack. The Nature Channel might want it caught on camera."

"Geez, thanks." I hang up and slide the phone back in my pocket.

"See how it's limping. I think that front right paw is injured," Denali whispers next to me, drawing my attention to the way the bear is favoring its foot.

"It can't be that old, maybe two or three by the size of it." I lean closer. "Sawyer need a new patient?"

"No." Her exclamation turns the bear to us, and he opens his mouth in a yawn.

I push her to the side, inching our way around the board. The bear isn't showing signs of outright aggression, no ears pulled back or woofing noises. I just don't like how the distance between us and him diminishes with each step. If there's anything I've learned from my time traveling the world filming animals, injured ones are unpredictable.

We get to the end of the board, and I pull Denali behind me as I step back to put the board across the gazebo opening between us and the bruin. It won't be much of a deterrent if he decides to charge, but it might slow him down enough for us to get somewhere safer.

The bear stops and woofs. Denali places her hands on my back. They're trembling, and all my protective caveman senses that were already firing jump to super-hero level. I wrap my arm backward around Denali and anchor her to my back. Nothing's happening to her, even if that means I have to wrestle this bear into submission with my bare hands.

Chapter Sixteen

-Denali-

There's a bear. A big, freaking bear. I don't care that Drew says it's young. The thing is huge.

I've lived in Alaska all my life. Had encounters with bears while fishing and hiking. They've always either run the other way when they realized I was there or not given a rip and did their thing.

This bear?

Nope, this bear acts like it just found an easy dinner with the way he's getting closer. Thank God, Sawyer and the dogs are inside. Lazarus would fight, and Hank would jump in. It wouldn't be pretty. Not with this beast injured and smelling like death.

I lift to my tiptoes to peek over Drew's shoulder. The bear makes eye contact. His beady, black gaze stares right at me. He woofs loud, stomps the ground with his good paw, and jumps our direction twice in a charge.

"Crikey, he does not like you." Drew adjusts his hold on me, gripping the back of my shirt in his fist. "Better stay behind me."

I slowly lower behind Drew and press my forehead between his shoulder blades. The bear woofs louder. Dirt flies out to the side of the gazebo in a puff as the bear shows his aggression. I flinch, letting out a shuddering breath.

What if the bear charges? I glance around. There's a woodshed about fifty yards away we might be able to get behind. It's toward the house, though, and I don't want to take the chance the dogs will get out. We don't make it to the shed, and there's a good chance my son will see me eaten alive if I go closer to the house.

I shake the thought off. We aren't going to be bear food. Not if I can help it.

The animal huffs. His steps scratch closer through the dirt. Drew backs up with slow, deliberate movements.

We're a unit. Pressed together like we are with him anchoring me behind him, it should be awkward to move. It's not. More like we're dancing, flowing together without thought.

It's grounding having the pressure of his strong arm around me. Feeling the way his back muscles bunch beneath my palms. Heck, even how he smells of sweat, drywall, and the outdoors anchors me.

I know, it's crazy to be noticing. It's just, I've never felt protected like this. Never felt connected to someone like I am with Drew, and not just in this life-or-death situation. It's like, the last weeks with him visiting Sawyer and shooting for the series has made me realize just how lonely I've made myself in my quest to be happy as an old maid.

His story of his mom and how she turned her back on love snagged right into my heart with a halibut fishing circle hook, dropping it fast like there was a two-pound weight on the line. I'm not so sure now that avoiding dating was about me looking out for Sawyer, or more about me taking the easy route, the safe road. What if in trying to protect Sawyer, I miss out on something that would be good for both of us?

The bear roars, and I wrap my arms around Drew's chest.

"It's okay," he whispers and threads his free hand with one of mine. "We've got this."

Not I've got this, but we've got this.

I believe him. I think the two of us could do just about anything. Drew has never been the cocky, alpha male I expected him to be. He's constantly putting people at ease, making sure everyone's included, even the animals.

The crunching of tires on gravel pulls my attention to the drive. Hopefully, it's animal control, and they have their tranquilizers locked and loaded. I squint as a bright yellow VW bug pulls in. The tires skid to a stop, and a woman with long blonde hair wearing a flowing dress pops out of the driver's side.

"Drew, get away from that bear." The tone is sharp, chock full of worry, and definitely Australian.

"Mum?" Drew turns his head, just as the bear stands, his head rising above Drew's shoulder. "Stay in the car."

Okay, the big brown bear is definitely not happy. I pull back on Drew, and he snaps his attention forward. My foot bumps against the decorative rocks lining the yard, and I stumble. Drew holds me even tighter.

Drew's mom's engine revs, and the pitiful beeping of

the VW's horn sounds. "You get away from my son, you beast."

A slap on wood cracks. The roof of the gazebo sways. The bear's going to charge, I just know it. A roar fills the air making all my muscles shake. Drew freezes, and his heart is pounding so hard I can feel it on my cheek pressed to him.

The bear huffs, and wood creaks again. I scan the house windows, finding Sawyer's face pressed against the screen. *God, please.* I don't want the last glimpse of my son to be in terror.

Sawyer's face splits into a grin, and his cheering bursts through my fear. I turn my head to find the bear running toward the bay. Drew's arm loosens, and my knees wobble. He spins and wraps both arms around my waist, his palms sliding up my back.

"We're good," he whispers low and rumbly. "He's gone."

I nod, since it appears my voice has vacated the building. His hand continues up my back, across my shoulder, and cups my neck. I'm trembling, but for a completely different reason, as I search his face. His forget-me-not blue eyes darken to the deep blue of the ocean before a storm. I want to dive in and never leave.

"You okay?" His thumb gently rubs my cheek.

"Yeah." My answer is all breathy like those stupid chick flicks Sadie loves to watch, but I can't help it.

All air sucks out of me with his stare. He trails his thumb over my chin, brushing my lower lip. His palm on my back pulls me closer, and all my resolve to old maidenhood evaporates. I'm gonna kiss him, just rise on the balls of my feet and lay one on him until he's weak in the knees too.

"Drew Leslie Wilder." His mom's shriek yanks me back to reality.

Drew cringes, then loosens his hold on me. I suck in a breath that's shaky and slightly desperate as I step away from him.

"Leslie?" I force a chuckle.

"Be nice." His hands drop away, but not before he lets them slide down my arm and spine, sending my skin into a riot of goosebumps—which isn't very nice, if you ask me.

"You said bears didn't wander willy nilly." His mom stomps up, her arms flailing and dress whipping in the breeze.

"No, I said polar bears aren't everywhere." He winks at me before he walks to meet his mom. "I didn't say anything about brown bears."

"Well, it's a good thing I'm here." She pulls him into a hug. "Maybe now I can talk some sense into you."

Her words hit like a kangaroo kick to the gut.

"Mum." Drew draws out her name like Sawyer does when he's exasperated. "What are you doing here?"

"You invited me, remember?" She clucks then turns to me. "He can be so forgetful sometimes." She smiles and extends her hand to me. "I'm—"

"Stella?" Vic's call from the backdoor of the house jerks Stella's gaze that way.

"Vic?" Now *her* voice is all breathy, and she fingers her necklace before tucking it into her dress and straightening her shoulders. "I didn't know you were here."

She shoots Drew a glare. I press my lips together to keep from laughing. She's definitely a firecracker like Violet.

Drew raises his hands in surrender. "He just showed up like you. Didn't tell me a thing."

"Looks like we had the same idea." Vic walks up all smooth and gives Stella a kiss on both cheeks. "You look beautiful like always."

She blushes and swats him on the arm. Dang, the man has skills. I peek at Drew, and he rolls his eyes and mouths, "Told you."

"Drew, I called Fish and Game for help." Sawyer skids to a stop. "They should be here any second."

"Great. Good thinking." Drew claps Sawyer on the shoulder.

"Did you see its front paw? It looks like it got stuck in a trap or something." Sawyer scans the area where the bear wandered to with his hand shielding his eyes.

"Yeah. I saw the paw, all right." Drew chuckles and looks at me over Sawyer's head.

"We should track it so he doesn't disappear before Fish and Game get here." My son's statement sucks all the levity from the situation.

Stella gasps. Vic puts his fingers on his eyebrows and shakes his head. Me? I just freeze like if I don't move, maybe the suggestion will slip away.

Drew clears his throat. "Sawyer, I'm not sure if—"

"I know you're going to go. I want to come too. We won't get close, just keep him in sight so he can get help." Sawyer spins to me, and I'm not going to like what comes out of his mouth next. "Please, Mom. That bear is hurt and needs a vet. If he disappears now, he might come up on someone else and not run away next time."

Why does my eleven-year-old have to be so grown up? Why can't he be happy with normal things kids like instead of being obsessed with helping animals, especially ones that could rip him in two in a matter of minutes?

I look at Drew. He's staring at me, quiet, willing to let me make the call. I know he'll keep my son safe. I also know I can't keep Sawyer from what he's meant to be.

My nod is quick and has Sawyer throwing his arms around me with a whoop. I close my eyes and squeeze tight. If I'm going to be willing to let go, to open life up to the possibility of more—more love, more fullness, more hope—I need to be able to trust. Not only Drew, but myself and Sawyer too.

Chapter Seventeen

-*DREW*-

Sawyer dashes into the house, leaving me staring at his mum. I can't believe she's letting her son go with me to track a bear that just about made us lunch. People here are proud of being Alaskan grown. Are situations like this what they mean by that? Where mums don't coddle their kids but let others take them on adventures so they can grow and learn? The weight of that responsibility and the trust Denali gives slumps across my shoulders like I'm carrying a humpback whale.

"You both are a couple of sandwiches short of a picnic if you think that precious child is going after a rabid bear." Mum's frantic voice pitches higher as she clutches the neckline of her dress.

"Mum, it'll be okay. We'll keep our distance." I check my phone to make sure it's got enough charge.

Don't want the battery dying when we're tracking a killer bear. Okay, that was dramatic. My mum is rubbing off on me.

"You're right. You'll keep your distance inside that

house. I don't understand why there's a need to go after the thing. Let the professionals do it. It's too dangerous, especially for a kid." Mum swats Vic's hand away as he cups her elbow to lead her inside.

"Sawyer's right. The bear needs to be followed." Denali pats Mum on the shoulder. "Don't worry. Sawyer's been around bears his entire life. He'll keep Drew safe."

She winks at me before striding to her car. I'm hoping she meant that as a joke, though the kid probably could. There is no way I'll let anything happen to him, even if it means we have to lose the bear's trail.

"No wonder you like this place so much. It's like those wild west movies you insist on watching." Mum leans her cheek on her hand and closes her eyes.

As welcomes go, this isn't the way I'd hoped her first visit would start. Denali marches back, spinning the chamber to her massive revolver. Mum flinches and bumps into Vic with a squeak. Her eyes go wide at the weapon.

"Do you know how to use this?" Denali's question pinches.

Sure, we have strict gun laws in Oz, but that doesn't mean I've never shot one. Granted, I've only shot at the shooting range, and it was an automatic. But it's the same. Right?

"Yeah." I don't think I convinced her if the rise of her eyebrow is any indication. "I've shot loads of rounds with a Sig at the range."

She just shakes her head and talks me through how her weapon works. I have to say, some guys would be put off by her explaining how to load a gun. Me? I find it enthralling and more than a little attractive. Maybe I'll let her give me lessons in shooting this particular gun later. Doesn't that usually involve getting close for instruction, or is that just in the movies?

"Are you sure I shouldn't let Sawyer take this?" She glances at Sawyer as he runs up with a can of spray paint and his backpack slung over his shoulders.

My manhood takes a hit with that comment, and I ease the gun from her. "No. I got this. I'm a good shot"

"Okay. Put the holster on, then go get 'em." She hands me the straps of leather slung over her shoulder.

I stare at it, my confidence waning. Maybe the kid should take the gun.

"Come on. We're going to lose him." Sawyer bounces on his toes, searching toward the bay.

"Let me help you." Denali takes the holster.

Stepping to me, she reaches over my head with the strap. I lean close, letting her steady breathing calm me. Her fingers tremble when she skims them against my side as she clips the holster on. She may be putting on a strong front for Sawyer and my mum's sake, but she's nervous. And why wouldn't she be? She's sending her amazing son to chase after an injured bear with a man she didn't know four weeks ago.

"I won't let anything happen to him." I whisper low so Sawyer can't hear.

She smooths her hand along the leather and looks up at me with complete confidence. "I know."

The trust she's giving me makes me bigger than Samson. I could take on a thousand enemy warriors with nothing but a donkey jaw. I could break a lion's mouth with my bare hands, but hopefully I don't have to prove that with the bear.

The desire to lean down and kiss her overwhelms

me, and the step I put between us is the hardest I've ever taken. I have her friendship and trust. For Sawyer's sake, that's gonna have to be enough.

I turn to Sawyer. "Are you ready yet?"

"Yes." He takes off across the yard, and I rush after him.

Mum grouses behind us about me being the death of her, while Vic promises to make her a cuppa. I don't look back. I can't. All my focus needs to be on what's ahead, finding that bear and keeping Sawyer at a safe distance. I can't let my mum's sudden arrival or the way Denali gazed up at me distract me.

I catch up to Sawyer and scan the area in front us. "What's the spray can for?"

He searches the ground, his look intense. "This grassy trail is hard to track with the way the stalks have matted down. I'm going to use the paint to mark which way we go so Fish and Game can move fast."

He points at a print half in the sand and half on the grass. I'd like to say I'd have found the track if I'd been looking, but it's so faint, I can't be sure. Sawyer sprays an arrow on the ground and continues toward the bay.

This kid amazes me more every day. Seriously. At this point, I'm more bodyguard than animal expert. And even in that, Sawyer could probably do better than me.

"Your mum ever take you shooting?" I keep my tone nonchalant as I adjust the holster.

"Sure. Grandpa takes me more, though."

Right. His chief of police grandfather. How could I have forgotten that? Wonder what he'll do when he finds out I took his only grandson after a rogue bear?

"I can hit a soda can at a hundred yards almost

every time." Sawyer stops and holds his hand over his eyes to shield them from the sun, scanning the horizon.

I just stare at the kid, completely humbled. "Mate, do you know how awesome you are? Seriously. I want to be like you when I grow up."

He smiles big before ducking his head. His ears turn as red as a salmon's belly. I love this kid so much I'd do anything for him.

A bear huffs in the distance, and I pull Sawyer into the taller grass. Sawyer takes out his phone, sends a text to his contact at Fish and Game, then pulls his binoculars from his backpack. For the next thirty minutes, as we wait for the cavalry to arrive, we watch the bear fish, passing the binoculars back and forth as we comment on different aspects of brown bears and what could've caused his injuries. It hits me as we talk. In all my travels and work with animals, none of my experiences meant more to me than this one.

Chapter Eighteen

-DREW-

"I knew there was a girl involved." Mum pushes me from her suitcase as I plop it onto Denali's spare bed.

"Shh, Mum." Could she be any louder?

"Don't 'shh, mum' me. I saw that look on your face after the bear left. You love her." Her shoulders jig back and forth in a happy dance. "You're going to make the most beautiful babies. Oh, and I get Sawyer as a grandson. Oh dear, it's too much."

"Crikey, Mum, Would you keep it down?" I peek out the door, praying Denali isn't walking up. "She'll hear you blabbing on. Besides, we aren't even dating."

"Why ever not?" She spins and places her hands on her hips.

"Because …" I'm not sure how to put this in a way that won't hurt Mum's feelings. Nothing brilliant comes. I lift my shoulder, and the motion feels like defeat. "Because I can't hurt Sawyer if nothing ever becomes of me and Denali. It's not fair to him, and I don't want to put him through that."

"Oh, please." Mum waves me off. "You and that girl have more chemistry reacting between you than that deluxe chem set I got you that one Christmas. And it's not just popping fireworks that fizzle, either. I'm talking slow-building, combustion type of burn. Speaking of, does this lovely little town have a Fourth of July celebration? I'd love a good Yankee festival."

"Holy moley, Mum, you're giving me whiplash. Yes, Seward has a celebration, and what does chemistry have to do with it anyway. You and Vic had it, still do, but that didn't matter, did it?"

It's a low blow, I know, but she can't be messing things up when I've done my best to just keep things friendly between Denali and me. Mum's face has lost its color, and now I feel like the biggest jerk in the world. I step up and pull her into a hug.

"Okay, you're right, I like Denali. I like her a lot, but there's more than just me and her I have to consider. I can't and won't be a disappointment to that young man. He means too much to me. He and Denali have this beautiful relationship. If I act on what I'm feeling for her and we don't get on, it might put a wedge between them. I don't want to be that wedge. I can't be more hurt to them than they've already had."

"Are you sure it's just about them, or are you protecting yourself?" Mum pulls back and puts her hands on my cheeks.

"Both, I guess." I might as well just tell her, so she'll drop it and move on. "Denali's it, Mum. I can feel it. The more I get to know her, the more everything inside me aligns into place. It scares me, more than anything I've come up against." I step back and push my hand through my hair to give it a good tug. "I don't want to end up like Vic, brokenhearted, but so in love with the kid and woman that I stick around. I don't want to be mid-fifties, lonely as all get-out, because if I let myself give in to what I truly want, I know there won't be anyone else but Denali, ever." I huff. "Shoot, I may already be past that point, but I can't let anything more happen than just friends."

"Drew—"

"All righty." Denali walks in, interrupting Mum, and my heart drops. "I've got towels."

Did Denali hear my confession? I give Mum a look, pleading silently for her to keep quiet. She pats my arm before reaching for the towels.

"I can't thank you enough for letting me stay here, Denali dear." Mum's smile is all charm. "I figured I'd just stay with Drew, but roughing it in a torn apart house just isn't up my alley."

"We're glad to have you." Denali's voice sounds off, like falsely cheery.

This is a bad idea. I'll just put Mum up in a hotel or something. Denali doesn't need to be dragged into my family's sudden appearance. Plus, who knows what my mum will say when I'm not around.

"I'm buggered." Mum sighs, the dark circles more pronounced as she gives me a tired smile. "Traveling always takes the wind out of my sails."

"Especially with such a long flight." Denali takes a step backward and motions down the hall. "The bathroom is just down on the left. Help yourself to anything you need. Truly. This is your home for however long you're here, so just make yourself comfortable."

Mum tosses the towels on the bed and closes the

distance between her and Denali. "Oh, sweetheart, thank you. You don't know what that means to me."

Denali leans into the hug, which surprises me. In fact, this entire situation has me wonky and unbalanced. Just over a month ago, Denali didn't want anything to do with me. Now, my mum is squatting in Denali's house for who knows how long.

"Night, Mum." I kiss her on both cheeks. "See you in the morning."

"Good night, darling."

I follow Denali out of the room and down the stairs. Her hair is out of her bun tonight, the ends waving in the middle of her back with each step. Inviting me to reach forward and run my fingers through it. Daring me to slide my hand along her back and pull her close. I inwardly groan and shove my hands into my pockets.

I never should've told Mum about my feelings for Denali. It's like the gates to the fish ladder have been opened and all those urges I've been holding at bay are jumping up the creek, trying to get through at once. Maybe if I get out of here fast enough, I can get my head back on straight.

Refocus on what's important.

Because what I told Mum upstairs is the truth. I'm so scared I'm going to mess things up for Sawyer. So terrified that if I slip just once, my heart will crack wide open and never close again. One step in the wrong direction is one too many.

We get to the living room, and Denali glances around like she's not sure what to look at. My mouth goes dry as the Great Sandy Desert. Crikey. If she overheard me—

"Your mom's great. I can't wait for her to meet

Violet." Denali's wringing her hands, her gaze hesitant when she finally does turn it to me.

"Yeah, thanks again for letting her stay. I'll find her a room or something tomorrow."

"Don't." The word is forceful, and she laughs. "Please, don't. That would be silly when we have the guest room and really don't mind."

Her fingers are curling and uncurling next to her leg, and I want to reach forward and stop the nervous movement. I step toward the door instead.

"All right. I know she'll like being here better than a hotel, so I appreciate it." I point my thumb over my shoulder. "Well, I probably should go."

"Yeah, okay." She follows me out, which I'm not sure is a good idea.

Distance is what I need. Distance and a healthy dose of reality. Seeing Vic sleeping on a cot back at my place should do the trick.

"Thanks for today. For letting Sawyer go with you after the bear. For, well, for acting like a human shield." She pulls the door closed and pushes her hair behind her ear.

"That was something else, wasn't it?" I stop a foot from her and yank my keys from my pocket so I have something to keep me busy.

"Yeah." She blows out a shaky breath.

"But we kept our cool and worked together."

"Yeah. Yeah, we did." She looks at me now, really looks. Her gaze pierces straight into the depth of me. "We make a good team."

My heart pounds in my chest so hard I'm sure she can see it through my T-shirt. I can't let my hopes leap too high. There are so many angles to that statement.

Me fixating on the one I want the most will just make it that much harder to keep the status quo as friends when her idea of a team and mine don't match.

"Yep. Bears are nothing against us." I twirl my keys once around my finger to release my tension. "Well, thanks for your help today and thanks for the pizza. Tomorrow we're shooting Hank and the car obstacle course, right?"

She nods. "Should be fun."

"As long as I'm not in a bite suit, it'll be a blast."

Her laugh is fast and loud, and she slaps her hand over her mouth. "Sorry. That's not funny."

"Fair dinkum, it's not funny, mate. I couldn't walk right for two days." I try to keep a straight face, but my lips don't want to cooperate, especially with her laughter floating between us.

"I'm so sorry about that. Really." She drops her hand, her eyes sparkling with mirth.

That's my cue to leave, because if I don't, I might just open the gate and follow my desires upstream. "Right, well, I better go make sure Vic is all tucked in."

Now, listen. Normally, I'm good at thinking things through before acting. I've managed filming seven years with wild animals in extreme circumstances without getting seriously injured or killed. My brain is always processing every minute detail so I can react, but, right now, standing this close to Denali, it decides thinking is overrated. It's the only explanation for me leaning in and tapping both cheeks with a kiss.

Her hand on my bicep and the way she tilts her head toward mine when I plant the second slows my leave. That leads me to mistake number two when I inhale the fresh, salty air that still clings to her. Vic had it right.

She's a siren, calling me to temptation.

I have to resist.

Can't be pulled in.

Moving away from the warmth of her skin is one of the most difficult things I've ever done. Now, all I must do is take that first step back. The next will be easier. It has to be.

"Drew," she whispers my name.

Her hands are on my cheeks, lips pressing to mine. There's no slow burn here. Napalm's exploding in my chest and rushing through my veins, consuming all thought but Denali. She gasps, her fingers skating along my scalp, leaving a trail of fire, before she pulls me closer and captures my mouth again.

My hands wrap around her. Skimming along her spine. Running through her hair. I've kept myself from any chance of touching her for so long, I'm starved for the feel of her.

She smiles against my lips, her joy overwhelming me in a wave of emotion. My knees buckle at the weight, and I stumble forward pushing her against the side of the house. My pulse pounds in my ears, mixing with our quick breaths and a dinging, like the universe is celebrating this moment with the ringing of bells.

"I've got it, Mom." Sawyer calls from inside.

Denali's gasp isn't charged with surprised release as before. Her hands push at my shoulders, and she breaks the most amazing moment of my entire life. I step back, chest heaving like I've just free-dived two hundred yards.

"The doorbell." Her words don't make sense.

"I could care less about the bell."

"We rang it." She tips her head back toward the house that we'd been pressed against, brushes her hands through her hair, and snags my keys from the porch. "Here."

I don't even remember dropping them.

A car pulls up to the curb just as the door swings open. Life rushes back into the bliss as Sawyer's eyes bounce between me and his mum. I swallow and nod at Sawyer.

"I was just heading out. Thanks for your help today, mate." I reach out to shake Sawyer's hand, praying he doesn't read any of the tension zinging between me and Denali.

"No problem." He smiles, grabs my hand, then throws his arms around my waist. "I'm so glad you moved here."

Okay. Wow. Too many emotions bottle up in me. Love for this kid. Want for more with his mum. Desire to finally have a family, a home. I just ... I just have to go.

Giving Denali one last lingering look, I pat Sawyer on the back, say my goodnights, and leave. There's too much hope in Denali's eyes for me to deal with now. I barely wave hello to Violet as she gets out of her car.

The need to talk to Denali is so crushing, I'm surprised I can walk away. Yet, with Sawyer still up and Violet just pulling in to visit, finding a moment alone with Denali will be next to impossible. Better to retreat, gather my thoughts. First, though, I think I'll take a dip in the glacial bay.

Chapter Nineteen

-Denali-

"What was that?" Violet grabs my arm as I come downstairs after telling Sawyer goodnight and drags me into the kitchen.

"What?" If I play dumb, maybe she'll drop it. Doubt it. At least I can root out what she saw and go from there.

"How about you kissing the world's sexiest man alive?" Violet arches her eyebrow and cocks her head.

Sure, Drew was awarded that distinction a few years ago, but he still owned it. Boy, is he hot. Not only that, but he's one of the most caring men I've ever known, which is so much more attractive than his looks. Lava-level heat rolls in my belly at the thought of him.

"It was nothing." I wave her off and skirt past her to the sink.

I need cold water, something to cool me down. Ever since I overheard him talking to his mom, ever since he said I was it, but he couldn't because of Sawyer, my brain has been in core overheat mode.

"Nothing!" Her glass-shattering loud shriek bounces through the house.

I shush her and look to the ceiling, praying no one comes downstairs.

"Nothing? Seriously?" Violet leans closer and points a finger at me. "If you think for one second that you are going to brush off the hottest, most toe-curling kiss I've ever witnessed, then you've lost brain cells. Probably burned them to smithereens while making out with Drew."

"Oh, no." I slam the glass on the counter and lean back against the edge. "Do you think anyone saw us?"

"Nah." Violet waves off my worry, opens the freezer, and pulls out the carton of Tillamook Marionberry Pie ice cream Drew had brought over. "You guys live on Lame Lane. All your neighbors are in bed by nine with dreams of prunes and gardening dancing in their heads."

She's right. Not that my neighbors are lame or anything, but they all tend to be older, especially the ones close. I probably don't have anything to worry about.

"What I want to know is when did you and hot stuff Wilder stop dancing around each other and actually acknowledge your attraction?" She digs her spoon in the carton and takes a bite.

"We haven't been dancing—"

"Please, you two have been acting like a couple of middle schoolers, all pretending like you don't notice each other, though that's all you notice." She takes another bite, closes her eyes, and sighs. "When did you stop buying that cheap ice cream that tastes like watered-down milk with artificial flavoring?"

"I didn't." I look at the carton.

I had no clue I loved the flavor until Drew brought it over. Now, my fridge has been stocked with it since. How did he know I liked it better than the rest? I never said anything. My fingers tremble as excitement and nerves overwhelm me.

"Drew brought that over." I stare at it, rehashing his words, thinking about little things he's done the last month. I tear my gaze from the carton and look at Violet. "What am I going to do?"

She's not the first person I'd go to for relationship advice. Probably wouldn't make it in the top five. She hasn't had a serious relationship ever. In fact, she hasn't had any relationships, more like a long-running series of first dates. But I am on the verge of an entire system meltdown, and I need someone to talk to. She looks up from the ice cream, her eyes widening in worry.

"Come here." She pulls me around the counter and shoves me onto a stool. Then she leans over the counter, snags a clean spoon from the drying rack, and hands it to me. "Eat."

I skim a layer of ice cream off the top of the carton she's placed between us. The cold, creamy bite melts on my tongue and slides a cool path down my throat. My hand trembles as I take another skim. She sits beside me, alternating bites with mine. Soon, the dessert has tamed the threat of internal combustion, and my body stops shaking.

"Okay, now tell me what's going on." Violet takes another bite.

"I don't know. Today has just been too much … everything." My mind spins through the day, making me dizzy.

"Take a bite." Violet clicks her spoon against mine, and it's loaded and in my mouth before I think about it. "Good. Now, why don't you start at the beginning and fill me in?"

So, I do, and not just what happened today but since Drew arrived in town. Of his initial flirting, then his complete one-eighty after meeting Sawyer. Of all the nights he's come over and hung out, not leaving me out but not coming for me. Of the bear, his words to his mom, and my oral examination of his lips on the porch.

"What am I going to do?" I set down my spoon. The click on the counter is like the cocking of a gun. I'm just not sure if it's signaling me to sprint ahead or aiming for a shot to the heart.

"What are you most worried about?" Violet pushes the carton away and leans her elbows on the counter so she can look at me.

"Sawyer."

"Granted, but what exactly about Sawyer are you concerned about?"

"That he'll get hurt."

"Okay, do you think Drew will intentionally harm Sawyer?"

"Never." My answer is out of my mouth before she finishes asking.

"All right. That's good. Why do you think Sawyer will get hurt?"

"Well"—I huff, rethinking talking to Violet about this—"obviously, I'm worried if we don't work out what that will do to Sawyer."

"You're right." Violet nods, her lips pushed to one side in thought. "Sawyer's pretty emotional about things. He probably isn't mature enough to handle it."

"He's not emotional." I gape at her as indignation sours my tongue. I imagine her bright teal and purple buns twisting into horns.

"Maybe, but he is immature. He'd never understand the complexity of adult relationships. I guess you're right to worry." She shrugs, her shoulders tight, and puts the lid on the ice cream.

"What are you talking about? Sawyer is the most mature kid I know. Heck, he's more mature than most adults, including you." I curl my fingers around my spoon, not entirely sure if I'm going to hit her over the head with it or just squeeze it to death.

"*I* know that." Violet rolls her eyes. "I'm just wondering when *you* forgot that fact."

Her words slam into me. My anger at her vanishes, leaving an odd vacancy in its wake.

"Sawyer's the most amazing person I've ever met." She points her finger to the ceiling with a jerky motion, her nostrils flaring. "Has been since he was a baby. He's so attuned to everything and everyone, like he's got these energy feelers that stretch out to the those around him and plugs in. He can tell when I'm excited or anxious and feeds me what I need. It's what makes him such a good vet. It's what makes him ten times better at life than all of us."

She shakes her head, grabs the carton, rips off the lid, and digs her spoon in deep. The bite is huge, but she shoves it all in her mouth. With a glare at me, she talks around the ice cream.

"You know what irks me? You do, and how you don't give him enough credit. All his life you've been all 'I'm thinking about Sawyer' or 'if I search for love, Sawyer will get hurt' or whatever hogwash you think up in your head. But the reality is that Sawyer wants you to be happy. He wants you to find love and laughter with someone."

Her anger surprises me. She's not typically grumpy like this. Violet's world is sunshine and rainbows with unicorns trotting around pooping cotton candy.

"Do you think he's too dumb to understand that sometimes things don't work out?" Violet jabs her spoon toward me.

"No. He's not dumb at all."

"Right. He's not. So how do you think he's going to feel when he realizes you kept yourself from even thinking about dating because of him?" Her words burn in my gut, making all that ice cream turn to acid. "How much guilt do you think he'll take on if he ever finds out you passed on someone you might actually connect with in an amazing way because of him?"

"How would he know?"

"He probably already knows. Feelers, remember?" Violet sets her spoon down again, penetrating me with a serious look I've never seen on her face. "Here's a question for you, what do you think will be worse, Sawyer's hurt or his anger when he realizes you used him as an excuse to cover your own fear?"

No, that's not what I've been doing. She has no clue what it's like to be a single mom. I've been protecting Sawyer, not feeding my own fear. At least, I don't think that's what I've been doing.

I stare at the counter and really think through my reasons for not dating. Yes, I always wanted what was best for Sawyer. Yet, skimming underneath that is a thread of apprehension that has nothing to do with him and everything to do with me agonizing over being left, again.

Of not being worth sticking around for.

Of being unloveable.

The sugary ball of creamed lead burns up my throat. I think I'll take my bubble gum Violet back now. Her words, while painful, are true. How could I use Sawyer like that? And not just with Drew but for the last eleven years?

I close my eyes, and a tear breaks loose and races down my cheek. "What am I going to do?"

Violet rubs the back of her fingers over my cheek, her voice back to soft and loving. "I think you're going to be brave, Denali Ann Wilde. Don't you?"

"I don't know." I squeeze my lids tighter as doubt and worry swirl in my mind and make my nose tingle.

"Well, answer me this. Do you like Drew? Do you think there's something between you two worth pursuing?" She pushes my hair behind my ear. "When you close your eyes and think of him, can you imagine life getting better with him in it?"

I really think about that for the first time since I met Drew. Every other time even a suggestion of a possible future popped up, I'd squash it from existence. No use living in what-ifs when I couldn't have them.

Now, though, I let all those imaginings free. I can picture Drew and Sawyer leaning over an animal, working together to figure out how to help or the three of us laughing around the table, playing a game or telling stories. Drew would support me in my dreams. He's already proven that. And now that I went and kissed the living daylights out of him, I don't even have to imagine how sparks will fly when we're together.

"I want to be brave." I look at her and take a deep breath. "I just don't know how. What do I do next?"

"Well, I say you repeat what happened on the porch. Just walk up to him and plant one on him." She wags her eyebrows at me. "I firmly believe that a kiss can tell you if you'll work out or not." Her words raise my own eyebrows to my hairline. "Mock me, but it's true. Why do you think I've had so many first dates and not so many seconds?"

I just shake my head, because I don't even know how to respond. It seems crazy, Violet on overdrive crazy. It also screams of Violet's own fear, like maybe there are no second dates because she's scared of getting too serious.

On the flip side, all the kisses I've had before Drew, even those with Nathan, may have been nice, but never had any fire. Drew's kiss? A rocket could've been launched to Pluto with how much heat that kiss produced. And not just his lips, either. The way his hands burned as they ran across my back probably left blisters.

"Okay." I sigh and lay my head on her shoulder, glad she was the one here for me after all. "I'm going to go for it."

I need to talk to Sawyer, though, tell him what I'm thinking, but me being scared and hiding is officially a thing of the past. Tomorrow, I'm kissing Drew again. Then, if he's willing, we'll see where things go.

Chapter Twenty

-DREW-

I made it home all right. Worrying, I know. Denali's kiss intoxicated my brain, having me zone out and swerve all over the road. I actually had to stop at Scheffler Creek and splash water in my face before I could keep driving. Yeah, the salmon fishermen got a kick out of that.

I turn off the engine and stare at my building. It's actually a house, and I'll be living in it for the unforeseen future, but eventually it'll be the clinic part of my rescue center. Maybe I need to look for an actual home. Isn't that the responsible thing to do? Buying one shows permanence, right? If Denali and I work out and she wants to live at her place, I could always turn my house into a rental.

I groan and push the car door open with a grunt. One kiss from Denali, and I'm wondering where we are going to live? Talk about being in over my head. I'm in trouble—thick, soul-drowning trouble.

I had commented my first week here about how

amazing the low tide was in the Turnagain Arm up toward Anchorage, that one could probably walk the width of it on seemingly dry land. A local shook his head and told me how people will venture out onto the sand when the tide is low, get sucked into the wet mire, then as the tide rises, drown a slow, agonizing death. Horrifying to imagine. Sends shivers up my spine every time I think about that. Am I one of the people right now, stepping onto inviting Denali-land, only to be cemented in when the tide changes?

Stopping on the walk to the back door, I stare across the bay at Seward. It's hazy in the dusk of the midnight sun. The lights of the town blink against the darkening sky, though it won't get pitch black until August. Fishermen, like dock pillars to nowhere, line the river's mouth. Their voices carry over the flat area beyond my back yard.

I hadn't considered the amount of people that would be positioned so close during the salmon run when I bought this place. It was really the only property near town that would work for what I wanted. Hopefully, I didn't jump the gun with this too.

I drop my chin to my chest and heave a sigh. After that scorching kiss, I should be flying on cloud nine right now, not drowning in worry. But I keep seeing the way hope shot through Sawyer's eyes the second he caught us on the porch. Keep thinking about how my own hope as a child had crashed when my mum left Vic. Instead of elation, I'm stuck with indigestion.

"What's bothering you, son?" Vic's low, soothing voice blankets over me, just like it always did.

I shake my head, not even lifting it. He steps up beside me and hands me a warm mug. Smells like chamomile, maybe a little peppermint. I snort a laugh and take a drink. Vic and his tea.

"Denali kissed me."

"You little ripper." Vic nudges me with his shoulder, his voice full of excitement. "So, why are ya out here, looking like someone died? Did the kiss not live up to your expectation? No spark, mate?"

"You kidding? It was like I drank from the elixir of life. All glowing and heat."

"What's the problem then?"

I sigh, trying to sort through my thoughts. "Remember when we watched *Indiana Jones and the Last Crusade* and that Nazi drank from the wrong Holy Grail?"

Vic chuckles. "You hated that part, screamed so loud when that man shriveled up to bones I thought I'd be deaf in one ear."

"Hey, I was only eight. That was scary stuff back then."

"Yeah, I probably shouldn't have let you watch it, with you being all sensitive and stuff." Vic sips on his tea, and I try to refute his comment. Since it's the truth, I can't deny it. "Your mum would've killed me if she'd known."

"Probably."

"How does that relate to you?" Vic leans back on the porch railing and crosses one foot over the other, settling in.

I might as well tell him. Maybe he can help me sort it out.

"I feel like at any moment reality is going to kick in. That I'll end up like that Nazi with all the life sucked out of me. But, unlike him, I'll still be alive." I toss the tea into the grass.

Vic sets his mug on the railing, his head bobbing in a nod. "I get that, especially with our past. You want my advice?"

"No, mate. I want to stand here staring at each other."

I cross my arms over my chest. I'm not in the mood for the back and forth. If I didn't want his help, I would've blown him off and pretended to go to bed. Vic just chuckles.

"When I met Stella twenty-five years ago, I never imagined life would end up the way it did. I'm not gonna lie. Her breaking off our engagement wasn't just the rough end of the pineapple. It was like my entire world had been uprooted, ripped clean from the ground."

"I know. That's what scares me."

"That's a real worry, for sure. The thing is, if I had the choice to go back and either not change a thing or never meet her at all, I'd still choose the path life has taken me."

"That's because you have a few roos loose in the top paddock." No way I'd pick that heartbreak a second time. I'm terrified of having it in the first place.

"Nah, mate. The thing is, I'd take the joy I have knowing you every time, even the scant beams of sunshine I get from your mum, over not ever having you two in my life. My life is fuller because of you. I've known true love because of Stella."

"Yeah, but you could've been with someone all this time. Had kids of your own."

"But they wouldn't be you."

Vic's strong declaration stings my eyes. I sniff and blink to hide the moisture. He straightens from the railing and closes the distance between us.

"Don't let the fear of heartbreak stop you from pursuing a relationship with Denali." He claps his hand on my shoulder. "There are a lot of things I regret with Stella, things I should've said or done to make things work out. Things we'll make sure you don't repeat with Denali. But I have never, not once in twenty-five years, regretted loving you or your mum."

He pulls me in for a hug, and I close my eyes to the overwhelming love he's always shown. I'm not sure what life would've been like without him. It's not something I've ever wanted to imagine. He's been my rock for so long, I'm permanently affixed to his steady foundation.

Can I be that for Sawyer, no matter what happens with Denali? I want to be, probably more than what's healthy for me. Is it too selfish to want a lasting love with Denali as well? I hope not, because I'm going to do everything possible to earn her trust.

Chapter Twenty-One

-Denali-

I peek at myself in the rearview mirror as I pull down Drew's wooded driveway and groan. Dark circles puff below my eyes. Since I hardly slept a wink, my face is fluffing its own pillows for my eyes to rest on. My hair is a nest of stringy red on the top of my head. I'm in that stupid Cookie Monster shirt again, because, in my determination to get over here and get this done, I threw on the first thing I grabbed. This shirt just bought its way to the donation bin. How is it always on the top of the drawer when I'm in a rush and not paying attention? Thank the good Lord I at least remembered to brush my teeth.

Glancing at the clock on the dash, I cringe. It's early ... like before seven in the morning early. My mouth is dry and sweat pools in my pits. Apparently, all my body's moisture is congregating there.

I slow the vehicle. Maybe I should just throw the baby in reverse and come back later? I could go home, take a shower, dress in clothes appropriate for an adult, then come back when I'm put together.

Drew's probably not even up yet. I stop at the edge of the forest where the drive opens up to his property. Pulling on the collar of my shirt, I stare at the house. If I leave, will I be able to work up the nerve to come back? We shoot the last episode today and celebrate with dinner at the Seward Brewing Company. Not talking to him now means we won't have time alone until tonight.

I wipe my sweaty palms on my leggings and swallow the wad of dryness stuck in my throat. I can't go through the day feeling like this, like I'll either throw up or pass out at any moment. I either suck it up and be brave now, or I might as well call in sick for the day, maybe the rest of my life. With a huff, I curl my fingers around the steering wheel and inch onto the property.

I catch movement out of the corner of my eye, and there he is, lifting an ax over his head and swinging it down onto a log, splitting it with one blow. He's tossed his shirt on the mountain of wood already chopped. His muscles flex and bunch as he flips the wood with the rest and sets up another log.

Two things register in my mind at once.

1. Drew is in much better shape than I imagined.

2. That winter's worth of firewood wasn't there yesterday evening when we left.

Every ounce of hesitation evaporates as his arms swing the ax again. Throwing the vehicle into park, I push open the door. All senses that my nerves had muted spring back to life in hi-def. An AC/DC song playing from speakers over by Drew comes to an end, and another I vaguely recognize starts up, the beat moving my feet forward. The morning fog smells of Sitka spruce and salt water and cools my burning skin.

Drew lifts the ax, his back and arm muscles bulging against his skin. The metal cracks against the wood, tumbling it off the chopping block. He bends to pick it up, turns to toss it, and freezes. This is it, the moment of truth.

Maybe it's lack of sleep. Possibly my constant replay of our last kiss. Could even blame it on the Aussie band's fast beat, but the moment Drew's gaze connects with mine, my pace picks up to a jog.

He drops the wood and meets me halfway where I skid to a stop. His eyes are full of questions as he scans my face, then slides into a blank mask.

"Denali?"

My chest heaves, and a mini-Violet shouts in my head to just kiss the man. So, for once, I throw caution to the wind and listen. I move in, sliding my hand up his shoulder and into his wavy hair. Rising on my toes, I press my lips to his in a slow, measured movement.

The music pounds with my heartbeat in my ears. He's frozen, not even breathing. My heart clenches, and I slowly pull away. What was I thinking coming here and throwing myself at him again? I should've never listened to Violet.

He grips my waist, his fingers flexing and yanking me close. His lips crash into mine with a desperation that matches my own. Warmth and hope flood into me, exploding my cells to life like they've been dormant, waiting all these years for this moment.

The song's lyrics are right. I'm thunderstruck.

His arms band around me, holding me against him like he doesn't want to let me go. My hands track down his cheeks, rough with stubble, and skim over his slick shoulders. He smells of pine and sweat, a testament of hours spent working even though its nearly morning. His obvious inability to sleep like I couldn't registers, making me wonder if he's out here because of thoughts of me or something else.

He's moving, lifting me up and carrying me away. His lips never leave mine, not that I'd let them. Next thing I know, my back presses against the woodshed, and Drew's mouth moves along my jaw, leaving scorched marks with each touch. Okay, I'll let them wander, as long as they are doing that.

I tip my head back, taking deep, quick breaths to clear my tumbling mind. We need to stop, talk things through, but the last thing I want is for him to let me go. He kisses up my neck, each contact igniting sparks that shoot straight to my core.

"Denali." His voice is low and husky and so dang sexy as his lips brush against my skin that I might just combust, catch the shed on fire, and burn it to the ground.

Reality crashes in like a tsunami. More than just this intense desire to be near him, I need to know what's between us. That what's happening here is not just pent-up attraction. I cup his face in my hands, slowing the kiss though everything in me is screaming not to.

"Drew?" I whisper against his lips, not even sure what I'm asking.

He leans his forehead to mine, takes a shuddering breath, then buries his face in my neck. He's still holding me up, pressing me against the shed. His breath heaves in great, hot puffs against my neck. My heart races in my chest, the beats skipping over each other. I tighten my arms around him, not willing to let a breeze of space come between us.

"Please—" He cuts off the word and squeezes me harder.

"Drew?" I run my fingers through his hair, willing him to look at me. I need to see him, to talk this through, so I don't dive into something that will leave both Sawyer and me disappointed.

Drew pulls back just enough to look at me. His gaze bounces back and forth over my face, searching. I desperately hope he finds whatever it is he's looking for.

I hold my breath. Maybe I should've just kept kissing him and not worry about talking. He swallows, his Adam's apple bobbing so much it had to hurt.

"Please." He leans forward, places a soft kiss on my swollen lips, and whispers hoarsely, "Don't break my heart."

Hope for our future bursts forth with my own worried thoughts skating from his lips. I kiss him, slow and long, the desperation of earlier replaced with certainty. If he's as scared as I am, surely that means what's happening between us is important and worth risking myself and Sawyer for, right?

Chapter Twenty-Two

-*DREW*-

Crikey. I'm dreaming. Must be. I'm passed out from exhaustion, and the thoughts of the night are manifesting in the most fantastical moment with Denali wrapped in my arms, kissing the living daylights out of me.

I inhale as she sighs against my lips. The sweet peppermint smell and the softness of her shirt as I run my hand up her spine to pull her closer gives me pause. I've never dreamed with all my senses. Which means this amazing moment is happening. That also means my pathetic plea happened as well.

My eyes pop open, and I pull back to really see her. Dark purple bruise circles under her tired eyes that gaze up at me. Her chest heaves as hard as mine, like we both can't catch our breath.

I rub my thumb across her cheekbone, skimming her velvety skin and cupping my fingers against her neck. "You're really here?"

"Yeah." She leans her head into my hand and exhales in relief.

"I'm not off with the pixies, lying somewhere, wool-gathering?"

Her flirty smile twists and twirls to my gut before she rolls her eyes and laughs. "I'd hope if you were thinking about me, you'd put me in something nicer than this silly shirt."

"Pull the other one, mate. This shirt is one of my favorites." I lean away from her but not too far. I want to make a point of checking out her outfit but don't want to go troppo and let her loose. I'm not crazy…yet.

She pushes my shoulder, but not very hard. My pecs flex at her touch. Which reminds me, I need to get a shirt on. I slide my hand down her arm, enjoying the shiver that races through her, and thread my fingers with hers. I may just be walking to the woodpile to get my shirt, but I'm not taking the chances she'll come to her senses and drive off just as fast as she arrived.

"You're insane. This shirt is problematic." She pulls at the hem with a scowl. "It manages to be at the top of the drawer at the most inopportune times."

As in when she's going to see me? I love the shirt even more now.

"It's going in the donation pile next time I wash it." She flicks the character with a huff, and I stop short.

"No. Please don't." Squeezing her hand, I unsuc-cessfully try to cover my desperation and play it cool.

"Why?"

"Because …" What wouldn't make me sound as ridiculous as I feel? Nothing comes to mind, so I lean closer, rubbing the edge of her sleeve between my finger and thumb. "Because the first time we hung out at your place, you were in this shirt." I slide my fingertips up the sleeve and along the collar, skimming the skin on her neck. "The moment you walked into the kitchen, your hair out of its perfect do and this silly monster on your shirt, I knew I had a problem."

"Why's that?" Her question is soft and airy like she's having a hard time breathing.

"Why? Put-together, all professional, and what not, you're beautiful. Intriguing." I kiss her on her neck along the collar. "Relaxed and totally at ease, you're stunning. Troubling."

"Troubling?" Her forehead wrinkles as she leans away to look at me.

"Fair dinkum, it's troubling." I snag her hand and continue toward the woodpile. "I realized at that moment that I wanted to see you in your relaxed state every day. I didn't want to only get to know put-together Denali." I drop her hand, snatch my shirt from where I'd tossed it, and yank it over my head. I shrug, trying to show a nonchalance I'm not feeling. "At that moment, I had to know all sides of you. Very troubling when I'd just determined not to pursue anything with you."

"Hmm." She fingers the hem of her shirt as she stares off across the bay, her teeth worrying her bottom lip.

I want to step up and stop her wheels from turning with another kiss. Another part of me wants to wait it out, hang back and build some sort of protection around myself. Like it or not, my embarrassing plea for her not to hurt me still reverberates through my soul, sliding as sickening doubt along the love and respect that's grown over the last month. I need her to work through her misgivings now rather than later, when there won't be a hope of me surviving in one piece.

"Why didn't you want to pursue me?" Her attention turns back to me, and, with a skill I didn't know I had, I remain still and don't flinch.

I blow out my breath I'd been holding and relax. "If my past taught me anything, it's that relationships mostly don't end in happily-ever-after. And, as attracted as I was and am to you, as much as you entice me for the first time in forever to give it a go, I didn't want to risk Sawyer being hurt." My gaze moves to the house behind her where Vic sleeps, and I huff out a laugh that totally calls me out. I've already begged her not to hurt me, might as well lay all my worries out for her. "And truthfully, I didn't want to end up like Vic."

"I wouldn't do that to you, agree to marry you, then leave." Denali's defense is immediate, another testament of how much stock she puts in being loyal.

"No. I know that." I run my hand through my hair, not confident in my agreement. "It's just, I knew that first night I met Sawyer that he was someone I wanted to be friends with." I hold up my hand in surrender as her forehead bunches in confusion and she takes a step closer. "I know that sounds like I've gone insane. Me, a grown man, wanting to be friends with an eleven-year-old. Probably makes me sound pathetic too. Which is true."

I close my eyes and shake my head. I'm screwing this entire conversation up. Denali's small hand slides into mine, and I heave a deep breath before looking down at her.

"The thing is, I don't want to jeopardize getting to know Sawyer, being someone he could rely on and helping him with his animals. I didn't want to disappoint him or get his hopes up. I didn't want the chance of not having his friendship if things didn't work out between us."

"And what about now?" She draws my arm closer, hugging it to her body.

"Honestly, I'm more scared than facing down that brown bear yesterday." I take in a deep breath and push a stray hair behind her ear. "But I also know I don't want my fear to cause me to miss something amazing, something I've always wanted."

"What's that?"

"You. Sawyer." I wrap my arm around her back and pull her up against me. "The chance at a happy family with two of the most amazing people I've met in the world."

Flog a dog! It's too soon to throw the f-word in the mix. Denali melts into me, burrowing her face into my neck and wrapping her arms around my back.

Then again, maybe letting my words get bigger than Ben Hur worked to my benefit. We're good for each other, the three of us. I know we can make this work, and I need to stop worrying.

I hold her close and let myself relax into this moment. She wouldn't be here if this wasn't going to work, wouldn't risk Sawyer's feelings if she wasn't planning long-term. Right?

Doubt tries to sneak back in, but I shake it away. Where Denali's thoughts about Sawyer are concerned, I know I'm right. She's not going to pursue a relationship with me and get Sawyer's hopes up, only to squash them later.

Chapter Twenty-Three

-Denali-

I grab mine and Sawyer's order from the barista at Resurrect Art Coffee House and head up the stairs to where Sawyer is waiting. After more kissing with Drew, sprinkled with a little talking about how we wanted to proceed, I can't put off telling Sawyer any longer. There's no way after the inferno Drew lit within me that I'll be able to pretend nothing's changed.

Besides, Violet's right. Sawyer's feelers probably already picked up on what's happening. I'll have to remember to thank her for the tough love moment.

Sawyer's texting when I get to the sitting area over-looking the coffee house. I love it up here. Love this place, period. The Rez, located in the old church, has this great vibe. Violet's bright paintings of the area hang on the walls next to other artists' stuff. I'm biased, but her stuff is amazing, so much so that sometimes I wonder why she doesn't do more with it.

"Who you texting?" I set down the tray loaded with

a cinnamon latte, a blueberry smoothie, and two cinnamon rolls so big we really should split one.

I'm eating the whole, dang thing. After worrying all night and making out all morning, I'm starving. Okay, we didn't make out all morning. It is pushing ten though, so … I fan myself with a napkin, heating up just thinking about Drew and his talented mouth. Maybe I should've gone with the iced latte.

"Dad." Sawyer sets his phone on the table and grabs his smoothie. "He says he likes his new team all right."

"That's good." I look at Sawyer over my latte, trying to pick up clues to how he's handling the change. "How are you doing with all that?"

He shrugs and shakes his cup. "Okay, I guess. Really miss him. Maybe when Frightful is bigger I can go visit him for a week or two? I bet Drew would take care of her for me."

"We could make that work." I'd hate it, with a passion, but if that's what Sawyer wants to do, then I'll buy the ticket tomorrow.

"Maybe. I don't know if I could leave the animals though. I mean, I know Drew can keep them healthy, but … I don't know." He sighs and sits back in the couch.

"We'll figure it all out later. No use worrying about it until you think Frightful is healthy enough for you to leave."

I really shouldn't be cheering in my head that he's so hesitant, but I am. I'm pretty sure Sawyer's desire will be to stay here where his animals are and the nature he loves is. However, there's always the possibility that the city will pull him in. I can see him sucking up all the culture and opportunities there and being too full to return. It happened with Nathan.

As amazing as Seward is, it's still a small town with little going on. Some people are meant for bigger things. Like Nathan … or Drew. I shake the thought out of my head. He's committed to being here, bought the property and everything. I can't let my old fears sneak back in. I need to trust Drew is serious about being here, for Sawyer's sake … and mine.

Pep talk firmly doing its job, I turn to Sawyer. "So, I wanted to talk to you about something."

"Is this about you and Drew making out on the porch last night?" His matter-of-fact words and nonchalant way he pops a bite of cinnamon roll in his mouth has me sputtering.

"We weren't making out." Okay, that's bordering on a lie. If we hadn't announced our kissing with the ringing of bells, that one scorching kiss probably would've escalated to full-blown make-out level.

"Please, Mom. Your hair was a mess, and Drew looked like he was caught red-handed doing something illegal."

I take a drink of my latte to hide my smile. Drew's expression had been comical, both shocked and busted. Completely adorable how he practically ran from the house. Come to think of it, I hadn't planned on jumping the poor man, so my expression probably matched.

"Then there's the whole post on the Seward Announcements group page."

I spew my latte across the table like a humpback spraying from its blowhole. "What?"

My voice carries over the busy coffee house, creating a pause in the noise as everyone looks up. I wave, then turn back to Sawyer, grabbing napkins and dabbing at the mess.

"That lady down the street, the one that guards her irises with a broom, posted a video of you and Drew. She said it was a public service announcement reminding everyone that the midnight sun didn't hide vulgar behavior."

Why, that nasty biddy. I'm seeing red. I don't think I've ever been so hot with anger. I snatch up my phone, determined to get the post taken down. Then, I'm going to rip up the nasty woman's irises.

"Don't worry, Rory already had it taken down. She came over all fired up. She and Sadie spent fifteen minutes on the phone, tracking down the admins of the group. You should've seen it, Mom. The post had over a hundred comments."

"You saw it?" Oh, dear Lord in heaven, kill me now. I try to remember just how carried away we'd gotten the night before, but my anger and mortification messes up my memory banks.

"There wasn't really anything to see. Even with her zooming in as far as she could, you can barely tell that you two were kissing." Sawyer shrugs and takes another bite of his breakfast. "Kissing isn't wrong. Spying is, though. Most of the comments were either cheering you on or telling the lady to mind her own business. When I took Lazarus, Hank, and Hope for a walk this morning, I had them do their business in her flowers."

I laugh despite the situation. This is definitely not how I wanted the conversation to go with Sawyer, and I'd be having a discussion with the neighbor about respecting others. It wasn't like Seward is a hopping place with paparazzi hiding behind every bush.

Would this little stunt bring people around trying to get a shot of me and Drew together? I've never really dealt with that before. Nathan's been able to keep his private life out of the news, so we've never worried.

"I guess I don't have to tell you that things have changed between Drew and me."

"So, what exactly does that mean?" Sawyer puts down his smoothie and leans against the armrest.

I don't want to sugarcoat things. Violet's right. He's too smart for that. I turn on the couch so we're facing each other.

"Truth? I don't know. I like Drew a lot, but we haven't known each other very long, and there's so much to take into consideration."

"Like what?"

"Well, you for one. Whether Drew and I can get along. Whether what we feel grows into more."

Whether I can trust that he'll stay. I can't tell Sawyer that item on the list, though.

"You don't have to worry about me, Mom. I'm old enough to know that it might not work out."

"Yeah, well, that still doesn't mean that it wouldn't hurt you if it didn't." I pick at the fraying hem of my shorts.

"I love you." Sawyer throws his arms around my neck, and I hold on tight. "You're the best mom ever, you know that?"

I'm not, not by a long shot. There's so much more I could've done to make Sawyer's life better. Sometimes I wonder if Nathan and I should have gotten married. We like each other enough and get along, things might have grown into love. I'd have hated leaving here and living the life of a sports star's wife, but at least Sawyer would've had a real family. Wouldn't be worrying about how he's going to divide his time. My eyes water, and I sniff and snag a napkin from the table.

"Shoot, Sawyer. You're messing up my makeup." I should've worn the waterproof mascara.

"You don't need it anyway. You're much prettier without it." As he grabs his smoothie, I smack a big kiss on his cheek. "Really, Mom?" His happy eyes dart to the stairs, then widen, his grin breaking out into a full-on smile. "Dad!"

He's out of the couch and across the room before I can even turn. Sure enough, Nathan's here, his arms wrapped around Sawyer in a hug that lifts him off the ground. My son's lanky body shudders as he cries into his father's neck.

Sawyer's tears show just how hard the separation from Nathan is on him and poke at the doubt I've tried to push to the back of my mind. If Drew and I don't work out or he goes back to filming his show, won't it be doubly hard for Sawyer? He might say he's old enough to understand, but his heart isn't invulnerable to breaking.

Chapter Twenty-Four

-*DREW*-

I pull into the training area, glad to find that Denali is already there with Hank. The crew should be right behind me, so any greeting I want to make better be done quick. After her visit this morning, I should be good to go on my need to be near her.

I'm not.

Not even close.

One look at her and I want to find a private place to get to know her lips better. She's back in her polo with her hair in a bun. I'm not sure what version of Denali I like more, the wrung out, kiddie T-shirt and wild hair Denali or the everything's under control Denali. Her approaching me in the soft light of the morning, exhaustion and hope mingled on her face, might be hard to top.

Maybe we just need to make more memories so I have a wide range to pull from.

I'm out of my car and across the field, eager to test my theory right here and now. She doesn't see me until

I'm a handful of feet away. Her eyes widen, and she pulls at the front of her shirt. I don't know what surprises her about my expression, but she better get used to it.

I grab her waist with one hand and cup her cheek with the other. Her palms press flat on my chest like she's getting ready to push me away. I kiss her tenderly, putting all those feelings I have too many of into the touch. It's not the passionate desire that dominated this morning. I'll save that for when we're in private. This kiss is packed with my banked hope for a future.

I skim my fingers along her cheek and trail them down her neck. Her skin is so soft, I can't help but follow my fingers' path with my lips. She shivers, and I smile against her neck.

"We have so much to do today." Her whisper shakes, and I pull her closer.

"Yep, we'll be flat out like a lizard drinking." I kiss my way back to her mouth, capturing her laugh at my phrase and lingering there longer than I should but not as long as I want to.

She pulls away and pats my shoulder. Her knees buckle when she steps away, so I wrap my arm around her back. You know, being a gentleman and all that. I can't help it if my smile is full of cockiness, not when I've left someone as amazing as Denali weak-kneed.

"What does that even mean?" She's staring up at me with a sparkle in her eyes, and I'm thinking this moment might be another favorite.

"What?" I have no clue what she's talking about.

She's smiling, her bottom lip pulled in her teeth. It's a triumphant type of look. Okay, so we're even. I may make her legs not function, but she blasts all coherent thought from my brain. Maybe between the two of us, we'll have one working body.

"Your lizard comment?" She steps away. This time her legs hold her up just fine.

"Ah, yeah, that. You know, so busy you fall flat with exhaustion." I shrug and bend down to greet Hank. Considering I spent the night chopping wood instead of sawing logs, that's exactly what will probably happen to me.

"All right." Her lips press together as she stifles a smile.

"What?"

"I don't know. Sometimes I wonder if you even know what you're saying."

"Maybe we just need to get you to Oz so you can see for yourself the vast array of expressions we Aussies utilize. It's quite impressive."

"I think I'd like that." She tucks her head, and her cheeks pink. Okay, if she keeps up that adorable blushing, I'll have to find a place to drag her off to and turn that blush supernova. She pats Hank and tosses him a ball. "You know, just to make sure you're not certifiable or anything."

"We'll just have to do that then. A mate of mine has a roo rescue Sawyer would love to see." I thread my fingers through hers, suddenly wanting to take her home, show her and Sawyer off.

"Look at us, making travel plans already." She swallows and looks toward the training course.

She's right, of course. We barely scratched the relationship status surface when we talked this morning, what with other things occupying our time together. If I want to prove to her that what is between us is more than just blazing heat that will die out, I can't just focus on the dream world full of sunshine and rainbows and grand plans of what-if.

"How'd your talk with Sawyer go?"

"Ugh." Her shoulders deflate, and even though my heart drops into my stomach so fast I might throw up, I want to make whatever went wrong better for her.

"That bad?" I squeeze her fingers.

"Not with Sawyer, no. He was all like 'duh, Mom. What took you guys so long?'" Her tone goes all exasperated teen, not like Sawyer at all, which makes the action even funnier.

I can breathe now, knowing Sawyer's reaction to us isn't the reason for her dejection.

"Remember that biddy I told you about?" She rubs her fingers across her forehead.

"The one who made the rude comment when you tossed your cookies in her flowers?"

"That's the one."

Denali glares off toward town, her eyes hard like she's contemplating murder. She's not a violent person, so whatever happened can't be good. Considering her dad's the chief of police, I'm hoping I don't end up going to jail for accessory, because whatever Denali is concocting, I'm a hundred percent behind. Except murder. I really couldn't go through with that.

"What happened?"

"She took a video of us kissing last night and posted it on Facebook."

I freeze, flipping through everything that happened on the porch. Doesn't take much effort for the reels to whiz past. It's all I thought about through the night. So much so, I had to chop four cords of wood just to get my mind off it so I could get some sleep. I roll my sore shoulders. Didn't help.

"Flog a dog!" I need to focus on the problem, not on Denali's propensity to kiss the living daylights out of me unexpectedly. If I want the latter to continue, I need to help fix the prior. "I'll go over there while the boys set up the shoot, talk her into taking the post down."

I've been putting on a good face for the public the last seven years. Surely, I can use some of that knowledge to charm an old, cranky bat into minding her own business. If that doesn't work, I'll bring my lawyer in. She'll slap Denali's neighbor with so much legal jumbo, the crank will back down.

"Rory and Sadie already took care of it. The post was deleted, but not before most of Seward watched it." She cringes. "Even Sawyer saw."

I snap my face to her, my neck cracking with the sudden motion. Now I'm replaying the kiss through the lens of an eleven-year-old. Embarrassment and slight horrification that Sawyer saw me practically maul his mum chill my body.

She laughs ... *laughs*! There isn't anything funny about this situation.

"Don't worry. He said you could barely see anything, which I verified with both Rory and Sadie. Also said he made sure Laz and Hope dropped a nice present in the nosey lady's flowers when he took them for a walk this morning."

I huff. "She deserves more."

"Yep." There's a possibility Denali's plotting revenge.

"Mom!" Sawyer's yell from behind us has both of us turning.

I jerk at the sight of Nathan Blaine, hockey all-star and deadbeat dad, walking behind Sawyer. Okay, from everything Sawyer and Denali have said, Nathan isn't like my father. He's actually trying to balance life in the spotlight and raising a kid. But trying and succeeding are two totally different things. I won't soon forget Sawyer crying his eyes out in my arms.

"Did I mention Nathan showed up?" There's something in Denali's tone that has my pulse picking up.

"Nope. Forgot to mention that." My teeth grit so hard together, I'm surprised I can talk.

Denali drops my hand and crosses her arms. "Well, he did."

"Great." Not great at all.

Denali peeks up at me, then heads to meet Sawyer. She doesn't look back or slow down. Her sure steps toward the two men that have dominated her life the last eleven years have uncertainty coiling cold, rigid fingers around my heart. Sure, Denali hasn't expressed any desire to be in a romantic relationship with Nathan, but when he pecks a kiss hello on her cheek, I can't help the bells clanging warning in my ears.

Chapter Twenty-Five

-Denali-

"Did I tell you I'm glad the filming's done?" My sigh comes from the very bottom of my toes as Drew threads his fingers through mine.

"A time or two." He rubs his thumb over the back of my hand, shooting warmth up my arm.

I can't remember the last time I held a man's hand. It's such a different feeling than holding a child's or mini-man's. The large palm pressed against mine and long fingers curling to hold tight makes me feel cherished. Protected. Silly to put all that in a simple touch.

The Sea Life Center is having some shindig tonight, so we are hoofing it to the brewery. I slow my step, wanting to draw out the pleasant walk before we're surrounded by people. Drew peers down at me, his eyebrows V-ing over his impossibly blue eyes. If I don't start talking now, I'm liable to throw myself at him ... again. He doesn't seem to mind, but I'd like to exercise some restraint, for goodness sake.

"So, when are Bo and Craig leaving?" The

cameramen have been such a constant the last four weeks, I'm going to be sad to see them go.

"Tomorrow. It'll be weird not going with them. We've been filming together from the start." There's a tinge of something that sounds an awful lot like regret threading through Drew's voice.

That touch of tone magnifies within me, making my heart turn into a razor clam holding its shell tightly closed. It's a dumb response, one I want to knock on the hard shell and tell it to quit. I mean, Drew's been with these guys for the last seven years. Of course, there's going to be some sadness in not going with them. As long as his excitement for here outshines the ache, we're good.

I pull him to a stop and slide my hand not encased in his around his waist. "Well, I'm glad you're not going."

"You are?" He pushes my hair behind my ear and trails his finger down my neck.

Seriously? I love how every little touch turns my body to liquid hot magma. I never, not in a million years, would've thought it possible. I mean, my favorite romance author, Bristol North, always has her characters overheating. In the past, I'd just laugh at how unrealistic that had to be. You can't possibly go through life in a constant state of meltdown.

Well, her novels are proving right, and I should've paid more attention to how the characters dealt with the heat rather than bingeing the book. One thing's for sure, if I'm going to be squirming with melted insides, Drew is too.

Yes, I'm kissing him again.

A searing kiss that boils over that magma coursing

through me and curls my toes. It's not even that passionate of a kiss, not like the ones last night or this morning, but the depth of the kiss, the way he cups my neck like I'm the most precious treasure, how he turns so his back is to the street, blocking us from onlookers, his grip tightening on my hand still threaded through his all have my heart pumping so fast and hard it's all I can hear.

I pull away, because if I don't, we might have another Seward citizen posting a public service announcement about the appropriateness of PDA. "Yeah. I'm really glad you're staying."

He stares at me, his eyes filled with so much yearning I almost don't catch the doubt lingering in the crease of his forehead. He rubs his thumb over my cheek, then drops his hand with a sigh. That lava flowing through me starts to harden, like it hit the cold ocean and is turning to rock.

A horn honks quick beeps, while a guy hangs out the window, whistling a cat call. "Get a room!"

I roll my eyes but can't keep the blush from heating my ears.

"You know"—Drew's mouth turns up on one side as he pulls me to keep walking—"I do believe Seward is going to be the greatest adventure I've had yet."

"Really?" My voice barely squeaks out, so I clear my throat.

"Fair dinkum. Nothing compares to the excitement of you." He winks, his words slowing the cooling process.

Maybe I'm paranoid. Drew's proved that he's sticking around in every action he does. It's not like he's at the same point in life Nathan was when he left after high school. He'd been shooting for his hockey dream, where Drew's goal has been his animal center. He's not going to bail on that before it's even started. Right?

We make it to the brewery without any more delays. Though, to be fair, there are some *delays* I wouldn't mind being interrupted with, but the streets are more packed than normal. I don't want finding pictures of us locking lips on the internet to become the norm.

The hostess's eyes dart between us before she giggles and takes us upstairs. A few people point as we walk by, then lean into each other, talking rapidly. Drew doesn't seem to notice. Maybe he's used to the attention. I need to let it go and not worry about what others say. I also need to forget about getting revenge on my neighbor for posting the video in the first place. I'm not sure which will be harder to do.

We reach the top of the stairs and can't help the smile that tips my cheeks up. I love how open the brewery has kept the seating up here. The floor-to-ceiling windows give amazing views of the bay.

Violet rushes over, her teal- and purple-streaked hair all curled pretty down her back. "Finally. We thought you guys weren't going to make it." She wags her eyebrows before giving me a hug. "When will we know if the network wants to do another season?" Violet asks as she gives Drew a hug.

"Don't know. I'll send today's stuff to them tomorrow, and we'll see what they say." Drew peeks down at me before heading to the table. "Of course, that will also depend on if you all want to do another season."

I'm not about to answer that question now. We barely finished filming the first season, and while it wasn't as bad as I thought it'd be, I really want to see what the network puts together before I agree to any more.

Sadie's here with Bjørn. Bo and Craig lift their pints to us as we approach. Violet plops back into her seat. Mark is talking with Rory, which isn't surprising, since she finagled a way to get him in a few of the episodes. Rory is all about spreading the network wealth to as many people in Seward as she can. Vic leans over to Stella and whispers something to her that makes her blush and laugh. Sawyer is sandwiched between Stella and Nathan. There're only two seats left at the table.

I slide into the empty seat next to Nathan, my heart full with a heaviness I haven't felt before. It's different than the normal weight of responsibility I'm used to. It's odd the way it's not heavy or cumbersome, but overwhelming in how it fills every inch of me. I scan those laughing and talking around the table and realize that for the first time in a long while I'm content.

It's terrifying, a feeling I'm not sure I can trust.

I lean my leg so it presses against Drew's. He squeezes my knee, but before he can move his hand away, I snag it under the table and hold on for dear life. His eyebrow rises in question, but I just smile at him. My inner tumbling doesn't need to cartwheel any further than in my mind.

Nathan bumps his shoulder against mine. "So, superstar, when does the series air?"

I shrug. "Fall, maybe spring. That is if they even like it."

"What's not to like? Four beautiful women in the wilds of Alaska. It's gonna be a hit, flocking people here just to get a glimpse of you." He jokes, but the words make my nose curl like I smelled something disgusting.

"I hope not." Violet pushes her hair over her shoulder. "Unless it brings cute men, then I might be okay with an influx. My options are getting thin here."

"That's because you don't take the time to actually get to know the poor men before you flutter off to the next." Sadie shakes her head, leaning into Bjørn.

"I don't flutter." Violet huffs. "I'm very strategic in my dating, I'll have you know. Besides, I'm still young. What's the use in getting serious at this point?"

"Just be careful with anyone new." Nathan picks at his napkin. "Fame isn't all it's cracked up to be. Brings a lot of"—his eyes dart to Sawyer, and he clears his throat—"let's just say interesting people."

"Weirdos. That's what he wants to say, Vi." Sawyer's matter-of-fact translation bursts the table into laughter.

Conversation mingles with good food turning the evening into one of the most enjoyable nights I've had in a long time. The waitress is clearing away our plates when I notice my friend Marie shaking her head at her husband. Her anguished expression twists something in my gut. I need to make a point of contacting her, maybe see if she wants to get a coffee or something. We've never been super tight friends, but since she married Chip, I don't see her at all anymore. She pulls on his arm, but he whips it away, making her flinch, then saunters over toward our table.

"Well, well, well. If it isn't the famous Wilde women." He sneers, swaying a bit as he stops. "You done making your 'documentary'?" He uses air quotes around documentary and gives a sleazy wink. "I know I can't wait to watch it if it's anything like the video I saw earlier today."

My halibut tacos curdle in my stomach. I'm not sure

if I want to throw up or deck Chip. Drew's hand curls into a fist on the table.

"Chip, please." Marie touches his elbow, but he ignores her.

"So, Denali, you getting wild with Wilder now? From one superstar to the next?" Chip's gaze darts between Drew and Nathan, and the air thickens with sickening anticipation. "Or maybe you're taking wild to a new level, hey?"

"Why, I never." Stella pulls Sawyer into a side hug.

Drew sucks in a breath and freezes, like a statue of stone doesn't move. I'm trembling, though I'm not sure if it's because of Chip's words or Drew's reaction. I twist the napkin in my hand.

Nathan stands, slow and deliberate. "You have an issue, Morris? I don't mind going outside and talking about it." The sharp edge to Nathan's voice causes fear to collect in my throat.

"Chip." Marie is on the verge of tears.

Chip stares at Nathan, the old resentment plastered ugly on what could be a handsome face. Finally, without a word, he pushes Marie out of the way and stomps down the stairs.

"I'm sorry." Marie wipes her hand across her cheek as she looks at me. She then turns to Nathan with so much torment, I want to start crying myself. "So sorry."

She spins and rushes down the stairs. How had she gotten tangled up with that jerk? Staring after her until she disappears, Nathan takes a deep breath before he sits. Drew still hasn't moved which is starting to slide an angry itch beneath my skin. I mean, shouldn't he be the one coming to my defense?

"Shame Chip never grew up." Rory huffs and pushes her glasses up.

"And that is why I'm not jumping into a relationship. Poor Marie." Violet shakes her head.

Nathan sets his hand over mine, stilling me from completely shredding the napkin twisting in my fingers. He leans over and whispers in my ear, "Don't let it get in your head and ruin your game."

I nod, quick and jerky. He squeezes my hand and turns to ask Sawyer if he's ready to go. While Nathan's reassurance is nice and all, I want to hear those words from Drew.

"Can we go?" I touch him on the arm, and he flinches.

"Yep." He stands and walks behind me to give his mom a kiss on the cheek. "Night, mum. Vic, see you at home."

My breaths are leaden in my chest, another new pressure I'm not familiar with. When we get to the sidewalk, I lace my fingers with his. The few seconds it takes him to curl his hand around mine bottle that pressure up my throat, causing my eyes to sting.

"Sorry about Chip. He's always been a jerk." I force the words through my tight throat, but, honestly, I shouldn't be the one apologizing.

He just grunts. I turn my head away, blinking my eyes to clear my vision. Pulling him to a stop, I squeeze his hand.

"So, what's wrong?"

I watch as all kinds of emotions cross his face. Anger and confusion are there, but the one that slams into my chest is the resignation dulling his eyes. That, I don't understand.

"You and Nathan are close." He's not looking at me but staring off over the bay.

"Yeah, well, we've been friends for a long time."

Where is he going with this?

"I'm surprised it didn't work out between you two, what with Sawyer and all." He looks at me then, and I see the jealousy hidden beneath the other emotions.

"We never loved each other, not romantically at least." I swallow and step closer, putting my hand on Drew's chest. "I promise."

He smiles, but it's full of sadness. I go up on my toes and touch my lips to his, hoping to reaffirm that what we have between us is what matters. Not our pasts or some bully's comments. While he returns the kiss, his hand splays across my back like he needs to use the width to hold me there. The weight settling between us taints the touch with a bitter taste of forlornness.

Chapter Twenty-Six

-DREW-

I stare at Vic's rental car as I pull up to Denali's house. When he left the house, he'd said he was taking a drive to think. I figured he'd cruise up the highway, not just across town.

What in the world is he thinking? Mum hasn't once, in all these years, opened the door to their relationship. What makes Vic think she'll do it now?

I park at the curb, shaking my head at Vic's bold move. Doesn't he realize pursuing Mum could blow up in his face? I shouldn't worry about him. I have enough on my own plate to deal with, like what's building between Denali and me and the fact that her ex seems to show up every time I come over.

Guilt and jealousy itch along my skin like dried salt water. Nathan is a great dad, so much better than mine ever was. I want Sawyer to spend as much time with Nathan as he can. I just ... miss Sawyer.

I slam the car door at my callousness and sulk up the driveway. What is wrong with me? My relationship with

Denali is amazing. The rescue center is coming along at a decent clip. Nature loves the show with the ladies and has offered an advance on another season, even though the first hasn't aired yet. Overall, things couldn't be better.

So, why am I walking around like a cloud of doom hangs low over my head?

The door to Denali's house swings open, and Mum's laughter bounces out. She waits for Vic on the porch as he closes the front door. When he extends his elbow to her, she sighs as she slips her hand in.

Geesh, Vic's not bold. He's dauntless.

Mum finally notices I'm walking toward them, and her smile brightens. "Hey, Drew."

"What are you two up to?" I step up and give her a kiss on the cheek.

"We're going to see if we can find some animals." Vic shrugs, and Mum playfully slaps him on the chest.

"Vic's taking us on an evening boat ride to find whales. Isn't that exciting?"

"Really?" I lift an eyebrow at Vic. He's really going for it?

"I thought Stella and I should experience this Alaska you've decided you love. See what the big deal is."

Sure, he did. It had nothing to do with a romantic evening on a boat.

"Violet's friend Kemp is taking us out." Vic pulls on Mum's arm. "He's waiting for us to get there."

"Well, have fun." I clap Vic on the shoulder, praying he doesn't get his heart broken again.

Knocking on the door, I wave at Vic and Mum as they drive away. I hope he knows what he's doing. The door swings open, and Denali smiles up at me. All worry over Vic vanishes under her smile. She grabs my hand, pulls me into the house, and kisses me hello. It's a tame kiss compared to some she's started, but it somehow calms the buzzing at the back of my head, the doubt and anxiousness that's lingered in the form of a headache since Nathan arrived. Like I know in my core what we have together is right, and her gentle kiss and warm smile settles that knowledge firmly over the negative.

"Mmm. I needed that," I whisper against her lips. "Might just take me another."

Pulling her up against me, her smile as we kiss pushes the rest of my anxiety away. I need to stop comparing Denali to my mum. They are completely different people with night and day motivations.

"Sawyer's been waiting for you to show up." Denali pulls me toward the kitchen.

"Only Sawyer?" I thread my fingers through hers and shake her hand.

Wow, Vic's boldness must've rubbed off. She just rolls her eyes and laughs. She'll keep me humble, that's for sure.

"Drew, come look at Frightful." Sawyer waves me over to the barstool where he's petting Frightful.

"Would you look at that, mate." I lean toward her for a closer look.

Frightful gazes at me, her head tipping from one side to the next. She stretches her wings wide and flaps. Wind and feathers hit my face.

"Crikey, she wants to fly." I wrap my arm around Sawyer in a hug. "Good job, Sawyer. You're brilliant."

"We got a hood and jesses from Marie Morris

today." Sawyer points to the leather strap around Frightful's leg.

"Marie? Didn't we meet her at the brewery?" I glance at Denali, and she nods sadly before handing me a glass of water.

"She said we're doing a great job imprinting Frightful to us," Sawyer continues. "She's totally comfortable with all this chaos, which is good for when Mom and I start training her."

"Mom? You're becoming a falconer too?" My eyebrows shoot up to my hairline.

Denali's forehead pulls low over her eyes. "Is that so shocking?"

"No, no it's not."

"Good. Sawyer, your dad's gonna be here soon. Why don't you put Frightful in her mew." Denali strokes the back of Frightful's head before Sawyer takes the bird outside.

"You know what I think?" I slide onto the barstool as Denali washes her hands.

"What's that?"

"I think you being a falconer is sexy." I wink, and Denali's cheeks turn a brilliant pink as she swats a kitchen towel at me. "So, you're going to learn from Marie, Chip's Marie?"

"Yeah." She glances out the back door at the patio, then leans over the counter. "I didn't want Sawyer out at their place by himself."

I don't blame her, not with the way Chip acted the other day. In fact, I'm not too thrilled with either of them being there. Not that I have a say in what they do.

"Maybe I'll take up falconry too." I stop myself from

saying more. Me getting all caveman-protective won't do any good. Especially since Denali can take care of herself better than I probably could. But I'm still thinking I'll find reasons to join them when training starts.

"Don't worry. We're meeting here most of the time." She pats my hand as Sawyer comes back in.

"She's all set." Sawyer beams at his mom, and I love the joy on his face.

"Hey, bud, you ready?" Nathan saunters in and gives Denali a kiss on the cheek.

Those caveman instincts I talked about? Yeah, they're on full-blown, chest-thumping mode. He extends his hand to me, and it takes all my restraint not to crush it.

"Nathan." I force a smile.

"Hey, Drew. How's the renovation coming?"

Here's the thing about Nathan, he's genuinely a nice guy. I want to hate him, but that's as fake as my smile. Sure, I'm not thrilled with him kissing Denali, but I'm also not Neanderthal enough to see it's just a friendly peck.

"Good. Slow, but I'm okay with that." I turn on the stool and lean back on the counter.

"I'll come out and try to help some this week." His offer surprises me. Why would he spend some of his precious time with Sawyer helping me? "You ready, Sawyer? I've got dinner in the oven."

"Yep." Sawyer hugs Denali, then me, causing my heart to do a happy jig. "See you guys."

Nathan waves, and the two of them head for the door. Confusion over Nathan's offer and Sawyer's hug tumbles in my chest like monkeys wrestling.

"I didn't hear Nathan pull up." I watch the door close and try to get some clarity.

"He probably walked. He only lives four doors down." Denali walks around the end of the counter and stands in front of me.

"Really?" Why does that bother me?

"Yeah. He bought the house about nine years ago so he can be close when he's here. His grandma lives with him." She shrugs, and the monkeys go into hyperactive level. "It works great having him close."

So, why don't I feel great?

"What are *we* going to do tonight?" She grabs my hand from where it's resting on my knee.

Her lazy circles on my palm spark along my skin and shoot up my arm, focusing those monkeys on one thing.

"I can think of a way to pass the time." I loop my fingers in her belt loop and pull her to me.

Her saucy grin as she leans into me blasts those sparks into my brain, booming loud in my ears like a fireworks finale and drowning out all my negative self-talk. She slides her hand up my arm and into my hair. I'm done with worrying. She wouldn't kiss me with such hope if she had doubts. Of course, the hope could all be on my end. *No thinking, just kissing.* I push the thought away and wrap my arms tight around her.

Chapter Twenty-Seven

-Drew-

Okay, so things have been plugging away. I've tried to let Denali wash away the doubt building inside me. She comes here to the rescue center to help when she's not training dogs. I go hang out at her place most evenings we aren't here. There's been mind-blowing kisses and lingering gazes, all the signs that the relationship is moving forward.

All things I should be chalking up as good.

So, why do I feel like everything is bigger than Ben Hur?

My thoughts race, and life is getting out of hand. It doesn't help that Nathan is around about as much as I am. I'm glad for Sawyer. Really, I am.

That's a big part of what has me struggling. The three of them joke and have fun. They include me, sure. But when I'm around the three of them, I feel like a third wheel.

Or, I guess that would be a forth wheel, maybe on a tricycle?

Whatever. It sucks.

Like I'm watching the quick end to my love story. It's not a happily-ever-after where I get the girl and a new life. Nope. It looks a lot like eventually the three of them will realize I'm not needed.

In a sick way, I'm glad for them. Yet, I stick around, because I can't get enough of Denali. Sawyer, either, for that matter. I'm bingeing before the abundance is stripped away, and life goes back to my lonely existence before them.

It also doesn't help that Vic and Mum's relationship seems to be simmering up to a boil. I want to warn him, tell him not to risk it. Because my anticipation of the hurt to come makes it hard to eat. I haven't slept well in days. There's a constant headache humming behind my eyes. I don't want Vic to go through the heartbreak of Mum leaving again. Why would he even consider wagering on a relationship that already proved a loss? From the looks of it, he is, and it terrifies me.

"Drew, can I get your help here?" Denali yanks on a tree where we're clearing shrubs.

We've been at it for hours in the heat. Though she's covered in dirt and her hair's in a crazy bun at the top of her head, she still looks gorgeous. I move to her side and eye the massive log. It's huge, but I'm gonna lift the thing. It might be my overcompensation for going up against the hockey super-star kicking in. I bend to heft it over my shoulder, but her hand on my back stills me.

"I have a better idea." She's wrapping her arms around me, sliding her hands up my back.

My lips are on hers a nanosecond later, drawing energy from her. That's how desperate I am. It's pathetic, really, but at this point I no longer care. I want what's best for her and Sawyer. While I had hoped and prayed it was me, the longer Nathan's around, the more I think them being a family would be better for them all. So, I have to draw as much from her as I can before she comes to the same realization as I have.

I pull her closer, fisting her T-shirt in my hands. Why couldn't I have listened to myself all those weeks ago? Why didn't I stay away from her with a ten-foot pole? Because when she finally realizes she's with the wrong guy, I'm done in. Might as well take me to the Arctic Ocean and drop me to the depths.

The only thought that keeps the ember of hope glowing in my chest is that Nathan will eventually leave again. He's got a contract to fulfill, after all. When he's gone, I should be able to solidify my status as the better bet for Denali.

Hopefully.

She pulls back and rubs her finger over my forehead. "What's wrong?"

"Nothing." Everything. "Just haven't been sleeping well is all."

"Why aren't you sleeping? Are you worried?" She kneads her fingertips along the base of my head and down my neck.

I lean my forehead on hers and close my eyes to the way her touch relaxes my bunched muscles. "No. Well, maybe." I huff out a breath and kiss her again. "It's more like Vic snores. No matter where I am in the house, I can hear him."

"Brutal." Her laugh blows joyfully against my lips.

"Yeah." Maybe all my worrying is as useful as an ashtray on a jet ski. Her kisses and touch certainly say my fretting is unnecessary.

"Better not tell your mom. Might give her second thoughts." And just like that, she dunks me in the frigid bay called Reality.

"Wouldn't want that." I hope the smile I push up doesn't look too fake. I step back and tip my head toward the garage. "I'm gonna go get the chainsaw. Don't think I can lift that tree."

She looks down at the heavy log and wipes her arm across her forehead. "Probably a good idea."

I wouldn't say I'm running away. It's called a strategic retreat. I don't want her probing any deeper, not when her joke about Mum and Vic hits like a thin, sharp scalpel sliding between my ribs straight to my heart. Tucking tail seems the only option that doesn't end with me blubbering all my emotions out.

"Drew?" Her call turns me around. "You don't have anything to worry about."

"No?"

Her smile is so wide, I can see her eyes sparkling though I'm a good six meters away. "This place is going to be amazing."

Right.

The place, not us.

"Thanks."

Now, I'm totally running away. Let's hope she thinks I'm just in a hurry to get the job done. She won't need to know that I'm pulling myself together while I "search" for the chainsaw hanging on the wall. My steps come to an abrupt stop when Nathan pulls in.

Like this moment wasn't already freaking me out.

His arrival twists that scalpel deeper and dumps a bag of sea salt into the gaping wound.

"Hey, Drew." Sawyer gives me a wave as he runs by to his mum.

"Hey, mate," I halfheartedly answer to his back.

Nathan meanders up to me, his limbs loose and relaxed. The exact opposite of mine bunched so tightly I can't move. He claps me on the shoulder in hello.

"Hey, man. Place is looking good." His gaze doesn't travel far from Denali and Sawyer.

I get that. They're all I want to look at too. We stand there for several seconds, watching Sawyer talk animatedly about something.

"I wanted to thank you for being here for Sawyer." Nathan shifts on his feet and crosses his arms over his chest.

"He's a great kid."

"Yeah. Me being gone hasn't been easy on him. On any of us, actually." He sighs. "But having you here and letting him help has made such an impact on him."

"I love having him around, mate."

I don't have the heart to say what I'm actually thinking. I'd like to tell Nathan that Sawyer shouldn't have to piecemeal his time with his father. Nathan's slump in his shoulders and downturned lips keep my mouth shut. As much as I hate it, I like Nathan. He's a great guy who's fun to be around. Nothing like my own dad.

"I can't do it anymore." Nathan pushes his hand through his hair.

"What's that?"

You know that feeling when you're standing before a dangerous animal and you don't know if you want to close your eyes or watch it charge? No? It's a horrible sensation that makes your skin chill with goosebumps, but your insides heat to the point all moisture evaporates from your mouth and leaves it dry. Your mind goes numb, probably to protect yourself from overthinking. That's what Nathan's words do to me.

"My whole world is here. Everything that matters, you know?" He motions to Denali and Sawyer, and I understand completely. "I should've never left, should've never been so selfish." He drops his hands to his sides. They're opening and closing into fists. "I'm quitting. Leaving hockey behind and coming home."

There's the blow I hadn't seen coming. My only chance exploding into a million little pieces.

"Crikey." I can hardly force the word out.

"I was going to wait to tell them until I talked with my manager, but I can't leave without saying something." He turns to me and extends his hand to shake mine. "Anyway, you know what it's like with these contracts and stuff. Pray for me that everything goes right, and I can get out."

"Sure thing."

He nods and runs to Sawyer and Denali. Nathan's talking, his hands shoved into his pockets. Sawyer whoops and leaps into Nathan's arms, but my eyes are glued to Denali, waiting for her reaction. She covers her mouth, her gaze darting to me, before Nathan pulls her into a hug.

I can't compete with that, with the whole happy family bit, can I? Even if she says there's nothing between her and Nathan but friendship, there was once enough chemistry to create Sawyer. With Nathan around all the time, eventually whatever sparked that reaction between them might ignite again. When that happens, I'm out. I guess now I have to decide if I stick around to the bitter end or cut my losses now.

Chapter Twenty-Eight

-Denali-

I'm not going to lie. Nerves have built a nest right in my gut. And not the variety that settle in and roost. No, these nerves are the swoopers. They fly in and out, twisting and turning in their coming and going. Distracting to the point where I can't get anything done.

Thank goodness it's the Fourth of July weekend and the only things planned are BBQs, the dance at the park, and watching fireworks shoot over the bay from Kemp's boat. If I needed to do something that required actual thought, I'd bungle it. Without a doubt. That's how distracted I am right now.

And all because of a man.

A stupid, ridiculously handsome man whose voice slides liquid warmth under my skin and touch ignites it on fire.

The man who in the last day has been acting all kinds of strange. I mean, there's been this kind of hesitance to Drew ever since the whole Chip incident, but I thought we'd gotten past that. We've spent almost every evening hanging out. Nathan even shared his news when Drew was around, which is still settling, by the way.

I never thought Nathan would just quit and come home. I'm hopeful, but a part of me is still wondering if his decision will stick. His entire life has been wrapped up in hockey since he was a kid. Can he even untangle from it and not get bored out of his mind? I'm trying to be excited for him, to support him in this change, but a part of me is very scared he'll be here for one season and decide it's not for him. It's not like he has some big plan like Drew does. If Nathan can't find his footing off the ice rink, will he just gear up and get back on? Then what would Sawyer think?

With all that to worry about, it's not what has my emotions flitting. No, that would be due to the big, Aussie bloke next to me who's been so distant all night he might as well have been down under. Sure, he and Vic picked up Stella and me, and we've spent the day wandering through the shops and tents set up for the weekend. He's even commented on how nice I look and held my hand as we strolled along. None of that means squat since he's basically operating on autopilot.

This is why I've avoided dating the last eleven years. Boys were hard to figure out in high school. They haven't gotten any easier in adulthood, either. Just bigger. And stronger. With piercing blue eyes that slice right to my soul and lips that make my exposed soul sing. I fan my face to tamp down the heat flooding there. Even confused as all get-out, the man still manages to have me searching the area for a private place to partake in creative communication.

"You okay? Want me to find you a drink?" Drew peeks down at me but quickly looks away.

He's pretending to search for something, but I didn't miss the way his cheek jumped in a slight cringe. I have no clue why looking at me is cringe-worthy, but it makes those nerves do a nosedive to my toes, leaving me light-headed. I shake the feeling off.

"No. I'd like to dance, though."

I point to the couples dancing in front of the stage where a local cover band is playing music from the eighties and nineties. Stella and Vic are swinging to a country song in an easy two-step. Her head tips back in a laugh, and Vic watches her with a satisfied smile on his face. I hope that Stella is considering a relationship with Vic, because from the look on his face, I'm not sure he'll survive her breaking his heart again.

I drag Drew to the dance floor just as the fast song changes to one of Jewel's songs from her first album. We Alaskan's love when one of our own makes it big. It's natural the woman on stage, whose voice slightly resembles the deep and soulful tones of Jewel, would sing one of hers. I just wish it wasn't the song *Near You Always*. The singer carries on about all the things she doesn't want her love to do.

Dang. Why couldn't the chick pick one of Jewel's other songs? I feel like the lyrics are all what I'm feeling for Drew bundled up in anguished notes and acoustic guitar. Drew's hand skims through the ends of my hair, then wraps around my sides, clenching me nearer. I'm holding my breath and trying to breathe at the same time.

The singer gets close to the end where the chorus is repeated. Her soulful singing sends shivers down my spine and brings tears to my eyes. I wish Jewel had never left Alaska and made it big. Then she wouldn't have recorded this song that's verbalizing all my feelings perfectly. I glance up at Drew to find him looking off into the distance, his cheek popping as he clenches his teeth.

"Drew?" My whisper drags his eyes to me, and I swallow from the intensity and resignation there.

"I need to talk to you." His voice tumbles out like hard gravel grating over my skin, and I want to slap my palm over his mouth to keep the words in.

"Okay. Talk." I press my lips together so I don't say anything else.

He glances around with a shake of his head. "Not here."

"No one's listening." I can't wait until we are somewhere else. If we do, I won't make it. I'm already on the verge of tipping into the emotional mess side of the scale.

He hangs his head, shoving his hands in his pockets. Those swooping nerves I was talking about? Yeah, they turn into hawks, big ones with sharp talons that are ripping at my insides. His entire chest heaves with a breath, then he looks at me, the hawks screeching warning in unison.

"I'm leaving tomorrow to shoot a show for Nature."

"Okay." Maybe this isn't as bad as I thought. "Is it an episode for the special you were filming when you first came here?"

"No."

All righty, then.

"It's a new series they want me to do." He finally elaborates, and it's everything I've worried about since the beginning.

"I thought you were done with that." My voice is small and so full of hurt.

"I thought so too."

"What about your rescue center? What about—" I shouldn't ask, but the words stutter out anyway. "What about us?"

"I don't know." His whisper is so low I can barely hear it.

"You don't know?"

I step back from him, trying hard not to let my voice rise.

"I—" He swallows hard and shrugs.

I close my eyes, a tear escaping and tracking down my face. I can't believe I did it again. Can't believe I opened my heart to someone who wouldn't stick around. At least I had learned some from my last go around with a bigger-than-life superstar and didn't let things go too far. Then the neighbor would really have a heyday about my decisions.

"I have to go." I take another step back.

"Let me drive you."

"No." I throw my palm up to stop him. "I'll find my way."

Alone.

Forever, it would seem.

Chapter Twenty-Nine

-*DREW*-

"I'm sorry, sir, but your flight has been delayed." The cheery woman at the airline counter makes a face that is part pout, part smile, and all fake.

"What do you mean 'delayed'?" I stare at her like she just gave me a complicated physics equation and asked me to find X.

I'm not dense. I've travelled more than most people I know. It's just I haven't slept since Denali walked away from me last night. Have hardly eaten. I'm pretty sure the pretzels on the plane from Seward to Anchorage don't count. So the airline worker's comment doesn't compute in a logical sense.

"The plane is having technical difficulties." Her smile grates on my tired nerves.

"When will it be fixed?"

I don't need this. I want space to think, and Anchorage isn't far enough. I'm not sure if trekking down to Oz would even be far enough. Too bad the dude from Amazon hasn't started colonizing Mars yet.

"We have our best mechanics working on it as we speak." So, she has no clue how long it's gonna take.

"Okay." I rub my forehead and pull the bill of my hat back down. "Is there another flight leaving today?"

"Let me check if there's room. It's summer, after all." Now her expression is frozen, but her fingers slap on the keyboard in impatience. "I'm sorry, but all the flights are booked."

"What about another airline?" I'm grasping now, my escape route closing quickly.

Click. Click. Click. She shakes her head. "Nope. Summers are a difficult time to fly in Alaska. Lots of people coming and going. I'll put you on stand-by if you want. It won't lose your place on your flight, but if something opens up before the plane is fixed, you'll be on the list."

"Thanks. I appreciate it."

I hike my backpack higher on my shoulder and stomp off. I should find a place to eat. Get some food in me. Maybe then I can think rationally and figure out a plan.

When I left this arvo, I told Vic I'd be back as soon as I could. Really, I shouldn't be leaving at all. There is so much work to do on the place. I've left it to Vic without so much as an explanation. Left without talking to Sawyer or my mum either. Overall, I've pretty much failed everyone that matters.

I blame that musician and her stupid song. I also hold my producer Steve responsible with his, "I've got a great show for you," call yesterday morning. The entire day, I'd coped well, considering my inner dialogue had been a complete mess.

Flying down to talk with Steve wasn't what I wanted

to do. Not really, but it had seemed like maybe I was thrown a life preserver, something that would save me from drowning in my anticipation of the inevitable.

Denali always does what's best for Sawyer. Always. So why would she pick differently when having a whole family would make Sawyer happy?

It was the question that had circled in my head since Nathan dropped the bomb that he was quitting. It distracted me the entire day with Denali, Vic, and Mum. The moment I would let my guard down and enjoy being there, Denali would do something that drove me out of my mind, little things like putting on chapstick, hugging my arm as we walked down the sidewalk, or laughing with my mum as she gushed over earrings made from fish bones.

I'm wild about Denali, completely in over my head in love. It must be better to break things off now before she leaves, right? I keep telling myself it'll be easier to heal my heart now rather than waiting any longer, but I don't want to let her go. Don't want to let Sawyer go.

I keep coming back to what would be best for them. I want to think that I would be, but then I remember how easy Denali, Nathan, and Sawyer are with each other. I just don't know if I can compete with that.

Honestly, I was doing fine. Sure, my brain kept waffling back and forth, but I'd determined to give the relationship a fair crack of the whip. It's why I'd gone to the festivities in the first place. Yet when Denali wanted to dance and having her in my arms sighing as she looked up at me, I lost it. All my fears folded out for me to examine—fear of Nathan coming home, fear of Denali's rejection, fear of that being one of the last times I'd hold her and my heart ripping out of my chest —I had to leave. Get far away so I can think.

Yeah, well, even now, everything in me screams to get back to Seward and hold Denali close until she forgives my boneheadedness. I find a corner table in the restaurant against the window and slump into the chair. If only the plane wasn't broken, then I'd be gaining that distance I so desperately need.

My mum's tone rings in my pocket, and I groan. I knew I'd have to talk to her eventually. In fact, I'm surprised it's taken her this long to call. I hate to say this, but as much as I love my mum, she's part of the reason I'm all messed up. I can't help but watch her and Vic and think that she's gonna break his heart all over again. When I asked Vic what the heck he was thinking, he just got this goofy smile and said some nonsense about his second chance at love.

More like second chance at loss, if you ask me.

Which he didn't, by the way.

I pull out my phone and groan again. Great. She's using FaceTime. I slip in my earbud—don't want the entire restaurant hearing her yell at me—and connect the call.

"Drew, what do you think you're doing?" She's frazzled, her blonde curls springing crazily from her ponytail. She doesn't have a stitch of makeup on, which is not like her at all.

"Hi, Mum. You're looking stunning today." It's the truth.

I think she might be more beautiful without all her makeup and hair done.

"She does, doesn't she?" Vic leans into the screen and pushes her stray hair off her cheek.

"You two are a couple of sandwiches short of a picnic." She swats Vic away, but her cheeks redden. "How I look has nothing to do with what the heck you think you're doing."

Dang. Couldn't distract her. "I'm going to have a convo with Steve."

"Why? I thought you were done with all that." Her eyebrows pull together.

"Well … I just think it's good to keep my options open."

"Did you break up with Denali?" Mum leans closer to the phone.

"Why? What'd she say?" My mouth dries out at Denali's name, so I chug some ice water.

"Nothing. I haven't seen her today." Mum slumps back and bites her lip. "But Sawyer said you told his mum you were leaving. I found the poor kid huddled with his animals in the back yard."

I put my hand over my eyes as my entire world spins. My throat aches so much a gallon of water won't help. I really should've talked to him before I left. What I should tell him never came, so I took the chicken's way out and didn't say a word.

"Drew, why are you leaving? I thought things were going so good." Mum's soft words cause the ache to burn even more.

"They were … are. I just … can't." I flop my hand on the table and gaze out the window at the plane landing.

"Why, son?" Vic's steady question pulls me back to them.

"Nathan's coming back." That should clear it up for them.

"Yeah, and?" Mum gives me a look like I'm an idiot. Maybe I am.

"Well, he …" I can't say the rest, especially with the look of exasperation Mum is giving me.

"You don't honestly think she's going to get back with him, do you?" Yep, Mum doesn't beat around the bush.

"It's what would be best for Sawyer." I point out.

"Whipus canus." She throws her free hand up in the air. "Vic, talk to him, because he's got more than a few roos loose in the top paddock, and I … I—" Her voice cracks at the end, and I know I must be the world's worst son at the moment.

The phone shakes as she fans her hand in front of her tearing eyes. I hate to see her cry. Spent my entire childhood doing what I could to make things easier for her so she wouldn't.

"It's okay, Stella." Vic takes the phone from her, props it against something so I can see them both, and threads his other hand through hers to stop her waving. "Drew, has Denali done anything to make you believe she'd get back with Nathan?"

"Maybe." No, not really. It's just a gut feeling I've got, but I can't tell them that.

"Really?" Vic's not buying it.

I drop my head with a sigh and shake it.

"I understand why you'd be hesitant, son. There's been some tough times in our past that would make it hard to trust that Denali wouldn't leave." Vic peeks at Mum before he continues. "I have one question for you."

I really don't want to hear it.

"Do you love her?"

Yep. Not the question I want to answer. They know the answer already, so it's pointless to lie.

"Yeah, but that just means it'll hurt even more when she leaves."

"Oh, this is all my fault." Mum places her face in her hands, her shoulders shaking in sobs. "I should've never let my fear trick me into running away all those years ago."

Both Vic and I freeze. This is the first time she's ever talked about what happened to make her change her mind. Her anguished look when she turns to Vic twists my heart.

"I'm so sorry. I was just scared. Scared I'd lose myself again, but more terrified you'd decide you didn't want me either." Her words are hard to make out through her tears.

"I could never leave you, Stella." Vic runs his hand down the side of her face. "You're my heart. My entire life. I've been here all this time, waiting for you to understand that there is no me without you."

They kiss, a soft, years of steady love kind of kiss. I should just hang up and let them be. Maybe by the time I get back, they'll be ready to get married. My thumb hovers over the end icon when Mum pulls away.

"Drew, don't be an idiot like I was. I threw away the best thing besides you that ever happened to me, wasted all these years we all could've been happy, all because I was afraid." She looks straight at me.

"I'm not—" Even I can't say the rest, because we all know it'd be a lie.

"Son, the worst thing I ever did was not fight for your mum. I thought if I just gave her time, she'd understand how much I love her." Vic's voice cracks. "Don't be like me, either. Denali and Sawyer are worth fighting for, even if you have to go against the hockey bloke. Because, you may think that what they need is Nathan, but maybe, what they really need is both of you. I don't think Denali's affection for you will easily be swayed. She doesn't strike me as that type of gal."

"Listen. I gotta go." I can't keep talking to them, not when everything they say screams to what I really want to do.

I tell them I'll call later, then hang up. Even though they might be telling the truth, I'm still not sure if my heart can handle the fight. I need space and time to think. There're really only two decisions to choose from. Do I take my chance and grapple for a life with Denali, or do I tuck tail and scamper back to my side of the world?

Chapter Thirty

-Denali-

"Oh. My. Word." Rory's shocked voice pulls me from my scrubbing. "Sawyer said it was bad, but I didn't think it was *this* bad."

I sit back on my heels and scan the spotless room. "What? I'm just cleaning."

"Where's Sadie?" Violet pushes past Rory, her head shaking as she takes in the living room.

"Camping with Bjørn. Why?" I lean against the cage I'd been working on and sniff.

I don't want company now, even theirs. I'm hanging on a frayed line, and at any moment it'll snap. If asked, I'll claim it's the cleaner making me tear up, not the fact that my heart got ripped out of my chest and destroyed like one of Hank's chew toys.

"We've come to talk about what's going on." Rory pushes her glasses up and steps into the room.

"There's nothing to talk about. I just got sick of living in filth." I sniff the burn of tears away. I really don't want them prying.

"Your house was far from filthy, and this is a bit over the top." Rory waves her hand to the DVDs organized by color.

"And what's with the depressing music?" Violet cocks her head. "I haven't heard Jewel in forever."

Okay, so listening to Jewel's first label on repeat might not have been a good idea. I should've gone with her later, more mainstream stuff, but since Drew said he was leaving, debut-Jewel has been the vibe I'm going with. It's chockfull of angst, and I'm definitely angsty.

"I happen to like Jewel, and I have cleaning to do, so …" I lift my eyebrow and motion to the door before turning to the cage and snatching up the toothbrush.

I scrub at nonexistent dirt in the corner of the kennel. The thing is now better than when we bought it new, but if I stop moving, I don't think I can hold the tears back. Even with the scouring, I'm on the verge of bawling my eyes out.

It's quiet behind me. If I just ignore them, they'll leave. Maybe. Oh, please let them leave.

The door clicks closed, and my shoulders slump a little. I held it together when I told Sawyer Drew was leaving. I made it through the inquisition of Violet and Rory, though I had expected more from them, frankly. Now, if I can hold it together to the end of the day, then tomorrow must be easier.

"I think you're done." Rory snags the cleaner from beside me.

"Hey!" Shoot. I knew that was too easy. I spin to grab it back from her.

"I'll take that." Violet yanks the toothbrush from my hand and tosses it over her shoulder. "We are having an intervention before you scrub the finish off the kennels and cause them to rust."

She pulls me up, rips my rubber gloves off my hands, and throws them with the toothbrush before I can even protest. Friends always joke that she's a bit too heavy on the artsy and lean on the substance, but Vi has grit. And apparently a lot of muscle. She has me up and walking to the kitchen without a grunt.

"Wow." She stumbles to a stop, her eyes wide as she takes in the kitchen. "This is bad."

"Worse than we thought." Rory nudges me to the bar stool.

"I don't know what you two are talking about." I plop down and roll my sore shoulders.

"Dee, the chip bags are evenly folded at the tops and"—Rory pulls the basket from the shelf with a nod—"the bags are alphabetized by flavor."

"So." Okay, that's overkill, but they don't need to know that.

Violet walks to the refrigerator. "The pictures on the fridge are lined up according to the date they were taken, and the state magnets … what?" She leans closer to examine them. "There's something here, but I don't get it." She turns to me and points to the offending magnets.

"It's no big deal. I just thought Sawyer would get a kick out of seeing the states in order of dates they were formed." I shrug and pick at the placemat we never use that I dug from the linen closet.

"We should've gotten here quicker." Rory's making a fresh pot of coffee, which is at least useful.

Violet opens the freezer and gasps. I cringe and close

my eyes, knowing what's coming. I probably shouldn't have organized the freezer.

"Denali." She says my name like I'm a petulant child who just broke the rules as she motions to the freezer.

"There is nothing wrong with wanting to be organized and clean." I cross my arms over my chest.

So what if it's not our norm. Maybe that's been the problem all along. If my life had been more in order, I wouldn't have been caught off guard.

"Yeah, sure, but this"—Violet swings her arms, motioning to everything—"this is going a little too far, don't you think?"

I don't want to think. Thinking leads to Drew's words. His words lead to emotions I'd rather not focus on right now.

Violet grabs the ice cream from the freezer, snags three spoons from the drawer, then joins me at the counter. Plopping the carton on the spotless Formica, she lifts the lid and hands me a spoon. I don't think I can eat right now, even if it is marionberry pie flavor.

"Talk." Rory takes the spoon Violet extends to her and digs in.

"I can't." My voice cracks.

Oh, no.

I can't break down now.

I set the spoon on the placemat. All the pain I've avoided by cleaning crashes over me. Closing my eyes, I take deep breaths to bring me back to a center I can handle.

"Why don't you start with what happened at the dance last night?" Rory's hand slides on top of mine, but I just shake my head. "One minute you were there, and the next Drew's standing alone, staring off down the sidewalk."

"It's nothing, really." I swallow the sharp wad of emotion stuck in my throat. "He's leaving, just like I knew he would."

"What?" they ask in unison.

"Guess Nature wants him to do a new show, and he agreed."

There. That was matter-of-fact enough. I take a long breath through my nose and brave looking at them. Their skeptical expressions have me wanting to snag the toothbrush and work on the garage floor…again.

"Tell us what happened." Rory grabs three mugs and fills them with coffee. "And don't leave anything out."

It's no use trying to get out of it. These two are wolves on a kill today. They'll keep at it until I stumble, then drag me down anyway.

I start talking, meaning to only tell them about last night, but everything spills. How hard I tried to just keep things friendly. His words I overheard to his mom. How he makes me feel more alive with every touch. His odd behavior after Chip's confrontation, and how he completely pulled away yesterday.

By the time I'm done, tears rush down my cheeks. The full ice cream carton is empty, and the coffeemaker brews a second pot. I just want to go to bed, pull the freshly washed sheets over my head, and never emerge.

"I don't get it." Violet shakes her head.

"What's not to get?" I toss my spoon into the empty carton with a huff. "I keep making horrible mistakes when it comes to men."

"First off, your relationship with Nathan was

completely different than what you have with Drew." Rory points her spoon at me. "You and Nathan were young, let your hormones control your actions, and were not even in love."

True, but it doesn't change the fact that he still left.

"Wait a minute." Violet grabs my arm.

I flinch. She's definitely been working out. I think her grip will leave a mark.

"When did Drew start acting weird?" She gives my arm a little shake.

"I don't know." I try to shrug away from her. "After Chip made that scene."

"After Nathan came to your defense?" Violet looks at Rory.

"After Nathan leaned in and whispered in your ear?" Rory's eyes widen behind her glasses.

"That was nothing, and, besides, Drew didn't freak out until yesterday."

"What happened the day before yesterday?" Rory's leaning over the counter toward me like I hold the answer to her riddle.

What she doesn't know is that I've already figured out the answer. In fact, there never was a riddle to begin with. I was foolish to think the outcome would be any different than it was eleven years ago.

"Nothing. I helped Drew at his place. Sawyer and Nathan showed up to help." I shrug, not caring anymore. "That's when Nathan told us he's quitting hockey and moving back."

"He's staying?" Rory straightens.

"Well, he had to go get everything finalized, but he plans to be back as soon as he can." I rub my fingers over my forehead at the headache building there.

"And he told you this while Drew was there?" Violet gives Rory another one of those looks. "That makes sense."

"Perfect sense." Rory nods.

I snort and go to stand. "Well, I'm glad you two have worked it out."

Violet pushes me back down onto the stool. "Denali, Drew thinks you'll get back with Nathan."

"What? That's ridiculous." Utter nonsense. "Why would Drew think that when I keep throwing myself at him? Literally. Every chance I get, I'm jumping in his arms and kissing him senseless."

Just the thought of his lips on mine and how he loves to skim his hands along my back has my toes curling. Stupid toes. I shift on the stool as heat races up my neck. Stupid blush. Don't they know that I can't react this way to thoughts of him anymore?

"It doesn't matter if it's ridiculous or not. Didn't you say something about his mom leaving Vic after they were engaged?" Violet pushes my shoulder again. "He's worried you're going to leave him like his mom left Vic." She taps her finger on the counter to make a point. "And what better reason to call it off than the father of your child returning home?"

"Oh, this would make a fantastic book." Rory presses her knuckle to her lips.

"No, it wouldn't, because it's insane. Sure, Nathan and I are friends, but I'm not ever getting back with him."

"Think about it from Drew's perspective." Rory points at me.

"I don't want to."

She continues anyway. "You and Nathan are friends.

Really good friends. How many exes do you know of that have a relationship like your's?" I open my mouth, but she keeps talking. "None, that's how many."

"It's not a bad thing to get along, especially not for Sawyer." I counter, not believing I need to defend my friendship with Nathan.

"You're right. It's amazing, but to Drew, it looks like the perfect recipe for heartbreak." Violet stands and paces to the pantry. "Think about it. Why wouldn't you just get back together and be a family?"

"Because I don't love Nathan like that." My voice cracks, and I'm going to lose it. "I love the dumb Aussie flying away."

"Does he know that?" Rory's question has me squeezing my eyes shut.

I don't want to cry anymore. "He should."

"But did you tell him?" Violet's back by my side, her hand sliding across my shoulders.

I shift my jaw to the side and shake my head. It wouldn't have made a difference if I had.

"I think you need to tell him, tell him that you love him and want him to stay." Rory reaches across the counter and places her hand on mine.

"No. I … I can't. I can't risk Sawyer being hurt." I try to pull my hand free, but she stops me.

"Can't risk Sawyer being hurt or you?" Her words cut, but this entire situation has me broken and bruised, so what's one more pain?

"Everything I do is for Sawyer. Everything," I whisper, the words bitter on my tongue.

"True. You're an incredible mom, but I think you're lying. This time I think you're afraid of risking your own heart." Violet kisses the top of my head. "Sure, Sawyer will get hurt if things don't work out with you and Drew. He already called us upset, but he has you and Nathan to support him, to help him. What about you, Denali? Will you be okay if you let fear keep you from a relationship with Drew?"

I gaze from one woman to the other, my heart pounding so hard in my chest it hurts. They're right, dang them. I can't keep using Sawyer as an excuse for hiding.

Drew's captured my heart and shown me what it means to love. If I let him go without a fight, I'm not sure there are enough toothbrushes and cleaner in the world to keep me sane. Besides, I'm good at holding things together by hard work and sheer will. I just need to figure out what it'll take to make the big lug realize he's the one I want, because apparently all the passionate kissing in the world isn't getting the message through his thick skull.

Chapter Thirty-One

-*DREW*-

I'd like to say that I got off the phone with Vic and Mum and jetted right back to Seward to find Denali yesterday afternoon. That would've been the smart thing to do. Apparently, I'm not that intelligent.

Apparently, I prefer to be miserable.

I sat in that airport restaurant and marinated in my misery for hours. My flight finally left, but I grabbed an Uber and found a hotel to sulk some more. You know that moment when reality hits and all the spinning doubt stills to a moment of clarity? Yeah, that was me, staring across the Gwennie's Old Alaska dining room when the waitress asked if I knew what I wanted.

Fair dinkum, I know what I want.

I want Denali and all the craziness that comes with her. She's the spark that's been missing from my life. I just need to convince her that I'm what's best for her too.

As soon as I find her, that is.

I've been driving around Seward since the moment

the chartered plane touched down. Her house is empty. The kennel is locked up tight. She wasn't at her parents', her aunt and uncle's, or the coffee shop.

I've driven up and down the streets, looking for her vehicle, only to come up empty. All the while the argument for her choosing me is building in my head. I may or may not have gotten concerned looks from citizens as I talked to myself while driving.

So now, I'm heading to the rescue. I need to check in with Vic and Mum and snag something to eat since I bolted from Gwennie's without ordering. Maybe they will have an idea of where Denali went. Since I can't find anyone, they could've all gone camping or on a search and rescue mission or something else entirely Alaskan. I can see Sadie and Violet taking Denali on an adventure to help her forget about the idiot Aussie.

If that's the case, I may just have to venture into the wilds of Alaska to find her. Or come up with a stellar plan to woo her when she gets home. Something like filling her house, every surface, with flowers. Ugh, cliché, I know, but considering I'm running on empty, it's all I've got at the moment. I'll just have to recruit Mum. She'll know what to do.

I pull off Nash onto my property, determined to make this check-in quick and get back to my search. The trees open up at the end of the drive to chaos. Workers swarm everywhere. Some I recognize, like Bjørn and Gunnar Rebel, but most I don't. I park behind the last car in a long line of vehicles filling my parking area.

Groaning, I push open my door. Vic must've dropped major bucks to get this crew here, since all the contractors I contacted were busy until next summer. I have the money but planned on keeping the bank account as full as possible for operating expenses. Vic exits the house, just as I'm about to climb the steps.

"What did you do?" I wave my arm to the people working in all parts of the property.

Maybe I should've eaten something earlier. I'm hungry, exhausted, and now, thanks to Vic, lean in the coffers.

"This wasn't me, mate." Vic holds up his hands in surrender, a ridiculous smile on his face.

"What do you mean?" A chop saw whizzes to life, making me cringe at the sharp noise. Did I mention that I have a splitting headache?

"Denali arranged a work party." Vic wags his eyebrows at me.

"You let her pay for all this?"

My heart leaps into my throat that all might not be lost with her at the same time as a wave of cold rushes over me. I dart my eyes to the insane amount of people working. It had to cost a fortune.

"No. She gathered up some volunteers. Why don't you go chat with the foreman?" Vic points to the wooded area behind the sheds where Denali and I cleared brush the other day. "I believe she's over there."

Everything else vanishes but the need to get to her. I walk across the property, then, when that's not fast enough, bolt. When she comes into view, I stumble to a stop. My chest heaves like I just ran the Mount Marathon Race at top speed instead of simply crossing the yard.

She's in that Cookie Monster shirt that I love, safety glasses, and earmuffs. The chainsaw she's wielding slices through the tree I never got around to moving. It's sexy as all get-out watching the sawdust fly as she expertly cuts a section off.

"Mom!" Sawyer calls from where he's waiting to help.

She kills the saw and looks to Sawyer, who points to me. Her eyes widen as she takes me in. I approach, stalking like a lion, never once taking my eyes from her. If I do, I'm afraid she'll disappear into the sea and never return.

Twigs and sawdust sprinkle her hair like homemade confetti. Dark circles mar her eyes, making me feel like the biggest jerk in the world. She lowers the saw to the ground, hesitation screaming in her jerky movements.

This is it. I have to get this right. Have to tell her all the reasons why we should be together. Have to make her see that life without her isn't life. Of all the times my words have mattered, this is the most critical. I get this wrong, and all hope vanishes like the morning fog. I stop in front of her, taking in the gold that lines her brown irises and how she licks her lips in nervousness.

Here we go. I open my mouth to state my case. "Hi."

That's it? One word? And even that came out all garbled like I have a mouth full of nails.

"Hi." She sighs, her eyes getting bright with tears.

I can't take it anymore. Stepping close, I wrap my arm around her waist and pull her to me. My lips are on hers, and relief rushes straight to my head when she kisses me back. My hand pushes through her hair, knocking off her ear protection. She fists her fingers into my shirt, pulling me closer. I want to kiss her for the rest of time, but I need to say what's on my heart.

"I'm so sorry," I whisper against her lips. Leaning

my forehead against hers, I cup the back of her head in my hands. "I let my jealousy and fear send me into panic. I should've never left. I should've told you how I feel." I lean back enough so she can see the truth of my words in my eyes. "You're the adventure of my heart, you and Sawyer. I could go anywhere in the world and never find happiness like I have when I'm with you. You're it, Denali Wilde. You're my start and my end. I—"

She stops my monologue with a kiss that has me off-balance. I teeter backward, but she spears her fingers through my hair and anchors me to her. She smells of Sitka spruce sawdust and salty air. Of home.

"I love you, Drew." She pulls back and looks in my eyes. "Please stay. Stay and build a life with us."

"I'm wild about you, Denali." I lift the corner of my mouth when she rolls her eyes. "I'm not going anywhere."

Just to prove my point, I put all my longing, all my love, into a kiss that would have the cranky neighbor blushing. All the world disappears except her and this moment. I came into the wilds of Alaska thinking I'd do a short segment and leave. I never imagined everything I'd ever dreamed of, everything I never knew I wanted, waited for me in this small, coastal town.

Chapter Thirty-Two

-Denali-

"She's a beaut, Sawyer." Vic leans over to Sawyer who has Frightful perched on his arm and runs the backs of his fingers over the feathers.

"She's growing so fast." Sawyer's pride in his bird is splashed across his face in a satisfied smile.

After finishing work at the rescue for the second day in a row, I told the family to come over for hamburgers. We're going to have a big thank you lunch tomorrow for everyone who came out. Tonight, I wanted to hang out with the most important people in the world to me.

"Who wants to lose at corn hole?" Violet tosses a bean bag in the air and points to Kemp setting up the goal boxes. "The reigning champs want to kick butt and take names."

"The only reason you won last time was because you cheated." Sadie shakes her head as she snatches the pink bags out of Violet's hand.

"I don't know what you're talking about." Violet's

shock is completely fake. She's always been a cheater at games, ever since we were kids.

"Reflecting the sun into my eyes when I took the winning shot? You cheat this time, and I'm dunking you in Sawyer's pool for the animals." Bjørn cocks his eyebrow before kissing Sadie on the cheek. "Babe, you ready to knock their tiaras off?"

"Absolutely." She plants a big one on his lips. "For luck."

Drew eyes me from the other side of the yard. Just the way he looks at me, like I'm all he sees, triggers tingles in my fingers and toes. I shift on the top step of the porch where I sit, determined to remain where I am. It's a herculean feat, but I really can't be running to him every time he gives me that look.

He saunters across the yard, never taking his gaze off mine. Those tingles ignite to heat that spreads through the rest of my body. This man is going to be the death of me, but, oh, what a way to go.

"Hey." He places his hands on either side of me and leans in to give me a lingering kiss.

"Hey." I'm surprised my voice works.

He spins and plops on the stair in front of me. Draping his arms around my legs, he leans back against me. I could stay here all day.

"So, Mum and Vic are definitely an item now." Drew's sigh scrunches my forehead.

"You aren't happy about that?" I massage my fingers along the tight muscles of his neck.

"Nah, it's good, but Mum's dropping hints that she's thinking about moving up here. Doesn't want to be halfway around the world from her future grandson." Drew leans to the side and smiles up at me.

"Oh, she's that confident, huh?" I raise my eyebrow as I shrug one shoulder. "Eh, we'll just have to see how her son woos her future grandson's mom."

"I'll give my fair suck of the sav." He threads his fingers through mine and kisses the inside of my wrist.

That simple touch really shouldn't affect me so much. Really. But here I am, drawing in a deep breath to try and slow my racing heart.

"I'm just not sure what Vic will think if Mum moves up here." His thumb traces lazy circles on my hand as he looks across the yard at Vic and Sawyer.

Vic's sitting in the grass with Sawyer next to him chatting away. Lazarus's tail thumps against the ground while his head lays in Sawyer's lap. Hope is curled up in Vic's lap. He's petting her red fur, completely enthralled with what Sawyer is saying. Pure love shines from the interaction.

"I don't think Vic will have a hard time deciding what to do." I hug my arms around Drew, cherishing this moment with family.

"I made lemon slushies." Stella raises a blender pitcher full of the drink … Sawyer's pitcher for his animals.

"Stella, wait." I try to untangle my legs from Drew's hold.

"They've got this special taste to them." Stella lifts her cup and drains half of it. "Quite refreshing." She goes for another drink.

"Nana—" Yes, Sawyer's already been told to call her that. "That's the blender I use for my mice and worms and stuff."

She freezes, cup against her lips and her skin paling.

Slowly, she lowers it and gulps. She straightens her arms to put distance between her and the blender and cup.

"Well then, that would explain the special taste. I think I'll go make another batch." She turns back to the kitchen.

"I'll help." Vic sets the fox gently in the grass and rushes up the stairs, squeezing my shoulder as he passes.

As soon as the door clicks, everyone left in the back yard bursts out laughing. I tip my head back and soak in the sound, the feel of Drew's body shaking in laughter against mine, and the joy filling the space like a hot air balloon preparing for takeoff. I squeeze Drew in a tight hug. I can't wait to see the adventure life with Drew holds.

Epilogue

-Violet-

Another cheer floats over the fence from the back yard to the porch swing. I'm sulking, I know. I just needed a break from all the gooey, lovey-doveyness happening back there. Not that I'm not excited for Sadie and Denali finding their soul mates and whatnot.

I am.

I'm also just a little depressed it's not me.

I mean, I've been on more dates than Sadie, Denali, *and* Rory combined. Not one has ended with a blip of connection.

No tingles.

No sparks.

Nada.

How is that even possible? I'm seriously d ·bting my philosophy on dating. This afternoon's disa: the perfect example. The super cute new hire at fo. tingle-worthy. Hot as all get-out and a complete sw. heart. The goodbye kiss should've had my toes curling.

They didn't even twitch.

Maybe I just need to take a break and test out the girls' nunhood approach. It obviously worked for them. Although, Rory hasn't had the same luck as the other two, but she rarely ventures from behind her computer or books. Kind of hard to find true love that way.

The screen door screeches open, and Kemp comes out with two glasses of lemon slushy. "Hey, poor loser."

"Whatever. We would've won if you hadn't bungled that last throw." I take the glass he hands me and pause it an inch from my lips. "This is a new batch, right?"

"Yes, ma'am. Sawyer cleaned his blender and put it in his room so there's not any confusion." Kemp's been in Seward three years, and his Southern twang still makes me smile.

He sits down next to me, and I lay my head on his shoulder. When Kemp showed up to a Search and Rescue meeting after just moving here, I never imagined I'd found my best friend. I have a lot of friends, but no one gets me like Kemp does.

Not that I've told him everything. I mean, he doesn't know the real reason behind my one kiss rule. No one but my family does. I push the thought away and refocus on the now.

"I think I'm taking a break from dating. I'm never getting married at this rate." I sip the tart drink, letting the coolness ease my nerves.

"Date wasn't great?" Kemp pushes off the porch.

"Meh."

"Same here." Kemp sighs. "I could tell she was way more into my status in the snowboarding world than me. Wouldn't stop droning on about different competitions I've done."

"Ugh." I'm down to one-syllable non-words. That's how out of sync I'm feeling.

"So annoying." Kemp takes another drink, an easy quiet falling between us.

"You know what we should do? We should move to a cabin in the wilderness and live off the land, leaving all dating behind." I sit up, a plan forming in my mind.

"Uh, no. We both like coffee from the Rez too much to do something insane like that." He shakes his head like I'm crazy.

"True." Though the thought of leaving everything and finding silence for a while sounds nice.

"At least, not right now. Give me a few more years of dating misery, and us disappearing might sound nice."

We sit in silence for a minute before he hums like his brain has hit on an idea.

"What we need to do is make a pact. Instead of disappearing, if we haven't married by the time we turn thirty, we marry each other." He turns to me. "Think about it. If it takes us six years to find our one true love, then we're a lost cause anyway and will probably be pretty desperate. I'd rather marry my best friend than someone who I settle for."

His logic makes sense but gives me pause. "Wouldn't we be settling with each other though?"

"Not really, at least not to my way of thinking." He shrugs. "We like to hang out and are together all the time anyway."

Okay. He has a point there. Though I hope it doesn't take me six years to find wedded bliss, having a back-up plan might take the stress out of the entire dating scene.

"All right." I extend my hand. "If we aren't ridiculously happy in love by thirty, we marry each other."

"Deal." He firmly shakes my hand.

We straighten back in the swing, and I sip my slushy. The lemon freshness and our pact lift my dragging dreariness. I may be the most free-spirited out of the four of us girls but having at least one guarantee in my future makes life a little more stable.

Will Violet's one-kiss rule prove true? Find out in Wild about Violet!

Acknowledgments

A book is never a one-person show ... at least not with me. There are so many people I want to thank, but then this book would be twice as long.

I'm thankful to God for the abundance of ideas popping in my head. I love how we as people are all so unique, and how He's given me this passion of writing love stories full of hope, respect, and courage.

I couldn't do any of this without my husband, Stretch, and his unwavering support of me. I knew I would marry him after our first date, and, over twenty years later, he still makes my core ignite and my toes curl.

I can't believe the amazing kids we have. Not only do they constantly ask me how the books are going or what story am I working on now, but they have become proficient at making themselves mac and cheese when I have my face glued to the screen for a deadline. They are my biggest cheerleaders, and the reason why I do this.

This book wouldn't have worked without the insight

of my Australian reader, Paul. He supplied me with Aussie terms so Drew didn't come across as cliché. Paul also bravely read an early copy of the book, giving me tips and corrections on how to make Drew authentic. There is no way I could have pulled this book off without his help.

Lastly, I wouldn't want to do any of this without my amazing readers. My favorite part of this business is getting to know you. I look forward to emailing and messaging you more than just about any part of this business. You are a blessing I wasn't expecting when I started writing, but one I cling to when the creativity or business gets rough.

Playlist - Wild about Denali

Near You Always - Jewel
Thunderstruck - AC/DC
Down Under - Men at Work
Need You Tonight - INXS
Someone Like You - Keith Urban
Can't Get You Out of My Head - Kylie Minogue
Alaska - Francisco Martin

Also by Sara Blackard

Vestige in Time Series
Vestige of Power
Vestige of Hope
Vestige of Legacy
Vestige of Courage

Stryker Security Force Series
Mission Out of Control
Falling For Zeke
Capturing Sosimo
Celebrating Tina
Crashing Into Jake
Discovering Rafe
Convincing Derrick
Honoring Lena

Alaskan Rebels Series
A Rebel's Heart
A Rebel's Beacon
A Rebel's Promise

Wild Hearts of Alaska
Wild about Denali

Wild about Violet

About the Author

Sara Blackard writes stories that thrill the imagination and strum heartstrings. When she's not crafting wild adventures and sweet romances that curl your toes, she's homeschooling her four adventurous boys and one fearless princess, keeping their off-grid house running (don't ask if it's clean), or enjoying the Alaskan lifestyle she and her Hunky Hubster love. Visit her website at www.sarablackard.com.

Made in United States
Orlando, FL
12 December 2021

11640242R00146